Heinemann
New Windmills

SIX MORE SHAKESPEARE STORIES

King Lear
The torment of a mad King who disowns one good daughter
in favour of two treacherous ones . . .

Hamlet
A ghostly visitation throws a young prince into a paralysis of
indecision . . .

As You Like It
A magical forest unites lovers and turns bad people into
good . . .

Julius Caesar
A tale of treachery, murder and revenge in Ancient Rome.

Henry IV Part One
The story of a young prince learning the difficult lessons of
kingship.

The Taming of the Shrew
The great battle of the sexes . . .

The most famous of Shakespeare's plays retold as short and
easy-to-read stories. Exciting, intriguing, amusing, Shakespeare's plays are brought to life by Leon Garfield's ideal
introduction to the greatest playwright ever known.

ABOUT THE AUTHOR

Leon Garfield was born in Brighton in 1921 and educated there. In World War II he joined the army and served in the Medical Corps for five years.

He lives with his wife, children's novelist Vivien Alcock, and is now a full-time writer.

Leon Garfield has won several awards for his writing and some of his books like *Smith* and *The Strange Affair of Adelaide Harris* have been televised.

LEON GARFIELD

Six More
SHAKESPEARE
Stories

Heinemann Educational
a division of
Heinemann Publishers (Oxford) Ltd
Halley Court, Jordan Hill, Oxford OX2 8EJ
OXFORD LONDON EDINBURGH
MADRID ATHENS BOLOGNA PARIS
MELBOURNE SYDNEY AUCKLAND SINGAPORE TOKYO
IBADAN NAIROBI HARARE GABORONE
PORTSMOUTH NH (USA)

First published in Great Britain by Victor Gollancz Ltd in 1985 and 1994

First published in the New Windmill Series 1996

96 97 98 99 2000 10 9 8 7 6 5 4 3 2 1

ISBN 0 435 12449 8

British Library Cataloguing in Publication Data
for this title is available from the British Library

Cover illustration by Chris Cody
Cover design: The Point

Typeset by CentraCet Limited, Cambridge
Printed and bound in England by Clays Ltd, St Ives plc

Contents

King Lear

Long, long ago, before even there were churches, there ruled a king of Britain whose name was Lear. He had three daughters; and when he grew old and longed to have done with the burden of governing and enjoy only the pleasures of being a king, he resolved to divide his kingdom between his beloved children, and keep only the crown for himself. Accordingly, he summoned them to his palace, and there, in the solemn council chamber, before all the dukes and lords and knights who could be crammed inside, he asked his daughters how much they loved him; for so much should they receive.

The eldest born spoke first: Goneril, Duchess of Albany, a great lady whose marble beauty melted into fondness as she told the world how much she loved her father. She loved him better than anything in the wide universe.

"Dearer," she declared, "than eyesight, space or liberty!" Then, with a rush and a rustle of wide skirts, she mounted the steps to the throne as a dark cloud ascending, and kissed her father's hand.

The old King, in his stiff robes like Time preserved in gold, gazed down at his kissed hand. What father owned a child as dear as Goneril! Proudly he stared across the crowding coronets that dipped and bobbed admiringly, a sudden breeze rippling a sunlit sea. Smiles stretched every face ... except for one! The Earl of Kent was frowning; and his plain face, in that tapestry of smiles, made an ugly rent.

Next to speak was Regan, Duchess of Cornwall, second in birth but by no means second in beauty. Her cheeks were stained with roses and her marvellous gown was feverish with pearls. How much did she love the King, her father?

"I am made of that self metal as my sister," she cried. "I find she names my very deed of love; only she comes too short..." Then she too mounted to the throne and kissed her father, not on the hand but on his withered cheek.

King Lear nodded, and touched the quickly given kiss as if it might fly away; and the web of wrinkles round his eyes glimmered as if with dew. What father owned a child as precious as Regan! Again the golden tide of coronets rippled with admiration; and again the Earl of Kent looked sour. Then at last that plain blunt man smiled. It was the turn of Cordelia, the youngest born, to speak.

In plain white gown, with no gold but her hair, and no jewels but her eyes, she stood before her father as her sisters had done, to offer him love in exchange for a third of the kingdom. Her face was grave and steady; and she said nothing.

"What can you say to draw a third more opulent than your sisters?" urged the King fondly, for Cordelia was dearest to his heart; and what father ever owned a child as true as Cordelia! "Speak."

"Nothing, my lord," she said.

"Nothing?"

"Nothing."

They stared at one another, he, bewildered into anger, and she, steadily, but with a thundering heart. She knew the world was watching her, and she felt her sisters' sharply inquiring eyes. She knew what was expected of her, but she would not, could not, submit. She loved her father as a daughter should, truly and with clear eyes. She could not swear, as her sisters had done, that she adored him as a god.

King Lear stood up, and the golden tide before him whispered and shrank back. Stretched smiles withered; the elder sisters slid their looks sideways; the youngest stared straight ahead. The King put his hand to his brow. There was a place that burned and burned, as if it would scorch his brain. It was the place that Cordelia might have kissed. He saw uneasy courtiers, with frightened faces, cowering back like cattle before a threatened storm.

But there was one who stood firm, as if he cared nothing for the King's wrath: the Earl of Kent. Yet his face, too, showed fear; but it was the fear that, if the storm broke, it would destroy father, child, King and kingdom alike. When private men act in anger, only private places tremble; but with kings, the whole world is shaken into pieces.

The King's eyes blazed, and his voice was thunderous. The storm had broken and the kingdom rocked with its violence. The Earl of Kent was swept aside, flung from the kingdom by instant banishment, for daring to step between the King and the object of his rage. Cordelia herself, not knowing whether she was waking or dreaming, swayed before the thunderbolts that were hurled at her from the throne. Her inheritance, her dowry, and even her father's love were stripped from her, leaving her trembling and naked of all that should belong to the daughter of a king. Then she was cast away. Two men had courted her: the Duke of Burgundy and the King of France. Contemptuously she was offered to them, with the nothing she had offered her father. Burgundy shrugged his shoulders and turned away; but France saw differently. He took her gladly, for, to him, her true heart and her honest soul were dowry enough.

Breathing deeply, the King turned to Goneril and

3

Regan, the daughters who had been dutiful, and divided Cordelia's inheritance between them. It was done. He had given up his power. He kept nothing back, but the crown itself and a following of a mere hundred knights. He relinquished even his palace; for with two such loving children, what need had a father of another house? Henceforward and till the end of his life, he would divide his time equally between the two he had so liberally endowed.

"Love well our father," said Cordelia, as she parted from her sisters.

"Prescribe not us our duty," came the cold reply.

Lately there had been eclipses of the sun and moon. A great darkness had fallen over the land, and beggars and wandering madmen had crept fearfully under bushes and into holes in the ground. Then had followed ruin and disorder everywhere, even in the royal palace, where the maddened King had banished Kent and cast off the good Cordelia. Surely the world was coming to an end! King against subject, father against child . . . and now, child against father! The Earl of Gloucester, another aged father in that motherless kingdom of Lear, on returning to his castle, learned that Edgar, his elder son, was plotting to kill him. Edmund, the younger, had told him, had even shown him a letter, written in Edgar's hand, in which the foul plot was as clear as day – if ever day was as dark as such a deed!

"O villain, villain!" groaned the Earl wringing his hands in dismay. "Unnatural, detested, brutish villain!"

Then Edmund, clever, handsome Edmund, laid a comforting hand upon his father's sleeve, and went in search of Edgar, to warn him, brother to brother, that their father, for some unknown cause, was in a violent passion with him, that Edgar's very life was in danger, and that, until Edmund could bring the Earl to reason, it would be best if Edgar fled.

Edgar, as noble and as foolishly honest in his way as Cordelia had been in hers, trusted his brother and believed his every word. Horribly bewildered and distressed, he ran from his father's house like a thief.

Edmund smiled as he watched him go. He despised and envied his brother, who was legitimate and so would inherit everything. He himself was merely the offspring of his father's casual lust, and would get nothing unless he shifted for himself. "Let me," he murmured softly, "if not by birth, have lands by wit." He himself had written the letter and invented the plot.

King Lear rode through the night. High upon a huge dark horse, the ancient King, cloaked and hooded in furs and heavy velvet, galloped across heath and common, through startled village and frightened hamlet, with his hundred knights streaming after, and a queer little patched figure, with face as white as paint, clinging to his back like a tattered hump. It was his Fool, his beloved Fool, who mocked at his madness, jeered at his folly, and yet was a thousand times more dear to him than any child. Goneril hated him; but her hatred was as a candle beside the furnace of hatred that raged within Lear against his eldest born.

She had scorned him! She had diminished him! She had told her servants to be insolent with him! She had commanded him to halve the number of his followers! He was no more than a tedious, noisy old man, and she had driven him out with her contempt. In scarce two weeks the great love she had professed, while she stood before the throne, had dwindled into such cold ash! He had cursed her; for did ever a father own a child as vile as Goneril!

But there was always Regan, beloved Regan, who

5

had sworn that her love for him had ever been greater than Goneril's. So it was to Regan that he was galloping so fiercely – not to her palace, for she and the Duke of Cornwall had gone from there and were now with the Earl of Gloucester. This was strange, for he had sent a messenger to warn her of his coming; and still she had gone. He found excuses for her, as a father would, good excuses ... but why had his messenger, who had gone after her, not been sent back?

The Earl of Gloucester's castle reared up against the grim sky like a black thought in a dark mind. Outside the heavy, bolted doors, sat a man, patient and quiet, with his legs imprisoned in a stout wooden gaol. He had been there all day. He was the King's messenger, and he had been set, as if he were a common vagabond, in the stocks.

The Duke and Duchess of Cornwall had ordered it, even though the Earl of Gloucester had protested that it was an insult to the King to treat his messenger with such disrespect. But the fellow had been brawling. He had soundly thrashed one Oswald, steward to the Duchess of Albany, who had come with a message from sister to sister. It would have been an insult to Goneril, who valued Oswald even above her husband, the mild-mannered Duke, if her servant's attacker was not severely punished. So the King's messenger had been put in the stocks; and there he sat, with nothing but philosophy for comfort and company.

He was a roughly dressed, roughly bearded, roughly spoken fellow who was new to the King's service; yet when he had seen how Goneril had treated her father, he had been as indignant as if he had served and loved the old King for all his life. He sighed and smiled ruefully. He had indeed served and loved King Lear for all his life; but, in humble clothes and with bristled cheeks, the King had never known him. He was a good man whose rough disguise showed up, rather than hid, his blunt nature. He was the banished Earl of Kent who had come back to watch over his beloved master.

He had sent letters to Cordelia in France, telling how matters stood in the kingdom, how the land was in worse disorder than ever, how the Dukes of Albany and Cornwall were at odds with one another; and that her father suffered. It gave Kent no pleasure to see how his warning had come true. His only comfort, as he sat with aching legs and aching heart, was news he had had that a French army had landed at Dover with Cordelia in its midst. He shifted in his confinement and whistled to keep up his spirits. Soon, now, King Lear's distress would be relieved.

The Earl of Gloucester had also learned of the French landing, and had guiltily hidden away the letter for fear of the Duke and Duchess of Cornwall's seeing it. The old Earl's life seemed in as ruinous a state as the kingdom itself. Edgar, his eldest son, had been proved treacherous beyond all doubt, had fled, and was being hunted down. The King's messenger was in the stocks outside his own doors; and the Earl seemed no longer to be master in his own house. Wherever he looked, he saw the Duke's armed servants; wherever he wandered, he was confronted by the sharp Duke and the sharper Duchess, till he felt like an intruder everywhere. They seemed even to have supplanted him in the affections of his last consolation, Edmund his faithful son. Edmund was a good deal more with the Duke and Duchess than with his father, the Earl.

Then, like a storm on horseback, came the King! With his wild white hair and his wild white beard flying round his flushed face, like the sun in winter, he demanded to speak with the Duke of Cornwall and his wife, who had dared to put his man in the stocks!

Wretchedly, the Earl carried the King's command to his mighty guests; and still more wretchedly came back with their cool answer. The King stared at him in amazement.

"Deny to speak with me! They are sick! They are weary! They have travelled all the night!" he shouted. "Fetch me a better answer!"

"My dear Lord," ventured Gloucester, caught between the anger of his old master and the fierceness of his new, "you know the fiery quality of the Duke."

"Vengeance! Plague! Death! Confusion!" roared the King. "Fiery! What quality?" and sent Gloucester back once more, to fetch the Duke and Duchess.

At last they came, and the King's man was set at liberty; but the King scarcely noticed his going. His daughter had come to him, his beloved Regan; and what father owned a child as precious as Regan? His heart overflowed with love for her, and eagerly, he began to pour out, in tumbling words, like a hurt child to a fond mother, the cruelty he had suffered at the hands of her sister.

She stopped him. "I cannot think," she said coldly, "my sister in the least would fail her obligation."

The King faltered, swayed a little, as if the wind had caught him; and stared. Had he heard aright? And was this Regan, his warm, fond Regan, standing before him, this stony Duchess with her granite Duke? No, it could not be Regan; nor was it Regan's voice that was now so cruelly telling him that he was old and near to death, and that he was no longer fit to be master even over himself; that Goneril had been right to check and shrink him, and that he should go back and, on his knees, beg her forgiveness! It could not be Regan, and therefore he would not curse as he had cursed Goneril. It was some monster in Regan's shape, for this daughter would never have forgotten the love she'd sworn nor the gratitude she owed. She was not like Goneril.

"O Heavens, if you do love old men," he cried out, with a sudden rush of anguish, "send down and take my part!"

Goneril had come. With brilliant eyes and wind-red cheeks from travelling, she had rustled to her sister's side, and now they stood together against the old, old man. Then, while the Earl of Gloucester trembled, and the Fool turned his frightened acorn face from side to side, the two daughters, with cold, indifferent looks, and words of colder reason, crushed their father's heart and blasted his brain.

Despairingly, he rushed from one to another. He would stay with Regan, he and his hundred knights! No. Regan shook her head. Five and twenty was the utmost she would allow. Then he would stay with Goneril! Goneril had allowed him fifty, and that was twice Regan's love! No. Goneril shook her head. He had no need of five and twenty, or even ten, or five. Then Regan smiled. "What need one?" she said.

The world grew dark. Black clouds rolled and piled up in the sky, and faint lightnings began to throw up strange configurations, like monstrous, glaring faces, and huge clenched fists.

The old King was mad. He was shouting and raving and cursing his children.

"Unnatural hags, I will have such revenges on you both that all the world shall – " He clutched his head as if his brains would fly out. "I will do such things, what they are, yet I know not, but they shall be the terrors of the earth!" Suddenly he turned to his thin Fool, who was all that remained to him of his old royalty. "O Fool!" he wept, "I shall go mad!" Then, together, King and Fool rushed away into the coming storm.

Unmoved, his daughters watched him go.

"'Tis his own blame," said one.

"I'll receive him gladly," said the other, "but not one follower."

The sky turned black, and drops of rain began to fall.

"For many miles about there's scarce a bush!" pleaded Gloucester, forlornly hoping to move Lear's daughters to pity for the shelterless old man.

They shrugged their shoulders. In a world of reason, there was no room for pity. However harsh the lesson, their father must learn that he was now no more than a beggar with a crown.

"Shut up your doors, my Lord," advised the Duke of Cornwall, grasping the old Earl by the arm. "Come out o' the storm." Helplessly the Earl was drawn back into the castle, and the doors were shut with a dreadful sound. Then the sky exploded with wrath!

It was a night such as no man had ever known before. It was a night of glares and roars, of wild winds and hugely down-rushing torrents of rain, of sudden sights of a world in ruins, stark, bare and broken, thrown up blindingly fierce, then plunged into blackness again.

"Where's the King?" shouted Kent, streaming, sodden Kent; then saw him, running hither and thither, shrieking and shaking his fists at the storm for joining with his monstrous daughters to batter down his old white head.

"I am a man more sinned against than sinning!" he howled, in frantic protests against the horrible injustice of the elements, that blindly punished guilty and innocent, oppressor and victim alike. The soaked Fool, clinging to his mad master with a mouse-like grip, wailed for him to beg his daughters to let them back inside the dark castle, over which lightnings forked and glared.

Desperately Kent tried to lead them away, for the old King would have died in the storm. At first, Lear resisted; then his wits, which were flickering like a windy candle, grew steady, and he saw the shivering misery of the Fool, his only faithful child. "Come on, my boy," he urged with great tenderness, and consented to be led. "In, boy, you go first," he said, as Kent brought them to the best shelter he could find, a poor hovel, as sadly tattered as a beggar's pocket.

But it was not so empty. Within was another wanderer in the storm, another outcast from the castle. Edgar, the Earl of Gloucester's falsely accused son, had taken refuge there. But it was no longer the smiling Edgar of courts and fine clothes. Hunted and hounded and in danger of his life, he had hidden himself in a shape of wild and pitiful horror. A madman! A grinning, scowling, shouting, naked madman, such as the many who wandered the land and plagued the countryside with howls and shrieks and glarings in the night!

"Help me! help me!" cried the Fool, flying from the hovel in terror, as, after him, with staring looks and whirling words, came the madman! The wind howled, the rain pelted down, and a huge flash of lightning exposed the naked wretch, all tangled with scratches from the flaying of briars.

"Didst thou give all to thy daughters?" pondered the King, shaking his dazed and battered head. "And art thou come to this?"

"Who gives anything to poor Tom?" wondered the madman; then he and the King discoursed weirdly with one another, sense and madness coming and going, and, like the storm's flickerings, now illuminating, now plunging them into dreadful darkness.

"Look!" cried out the Fool. "Here comes a walking fire!"

A torch, hissing and smoking, was weaving through the night, and the Earl of Gloucester, fear and pity shining in his flame-lit eyes, came stumbling towards them. Although forbidden to help the King, he had crept secretly from the castle to find his old master and bring him to a farm-building nearby, where food and a fire had been prepared. "What! hath your Grace no better company?" he asked in dismay, when he found the King in deep talk with the mad beggar. He no more knew his son naked than he had really known him in his best attire.

But the King would not be parted from his new companion, so all followed the Earl as he led them, secretly, to shelter. "No words, no words," he whispered, as they drew near the castle. "Hush!"

"Child Roland to the dark tower came," mumbled the madman, staring up at the grim bulk. "His word was still: fie, foh, and fum, I smell the blood of a British man."

The room was humble, but there was food on the table and a fire in the hearth; there were rough country stools and a rough country bed, on which the Earl had laid cushions more fit for a King. "I will not be long from you," he promised Kent, and returned to the castle to see what else he could bring for the comfort of the broken King.

The storm was weakening; wind and rain dwindled, and the thunder sank to a grumbling. Kent begged the King to lie down; but he would not. He had important business first. His daughters must be brought to trial. Their crimes? Hard hearts and ingratitude. Their judges? The madman, the Fool and Kent. The King himself would give evidence.

"Arraign her first," he said, pointing accusingly at a stool; "'tis Goneril. I here take my oath before this honourable assembly she kicked the poor King, her father."

Kent turned aside, and even Edgar, the false madman, could scarce hold back his tears for the flickering ruin of King Lear's mind. Only the Fool, his spirits lifted by warmth and comfort, supported his master in his madness.

"We'll go to supper i' the morning," said the King, with a gracious gesture, as at last he lay down on the bed.

"And I'll go to bed at noon," said the Fool, fondly mocking his master's flourish and tone.

The King was sleeping when Gloucester returned. His face was pale, his voice trembled. Lear's daughters were planning their father's death. The King must leave at once. There was a cart waiting that would carry him to Dover. "Come, help to bear thy master," said Kent to the Fool, as he and Gloucester between them, lifted the still sleeping King. "Thou must not stay behind."

The King had gone and the naked madman had crept away. The night was quiet and a few faint stars pricked through the tatters of the sky. There was a sudden noise of horses, galloping, then it died away. The castle was dark, and its fanged battlements seemed to strike at the sky. The Earl of Gloucester, his act of mercy done, went back inside.

They were waiting for him, the Duke and Duchess of Cornwall. The Duchess of Albany and Edmund, his son, had left him to face Regan and her terrible husband. They had discovered he had helped the King; and worse, they had found the letter telling of the French landing and Cordelia's return.

He was seized by the Duke's servants and bound tightly to a chair.

"You are my guests: do me no foul play, friends!" he pleaded, staring up into the eyes where pity had never shone. For answer, Regan leaned forward and mockingly plucked at his beard. He cried out in shocked amazement.

Then the Duke began to question him . . . about the

King, about the letter. Why had he sent the King to Dover? He was a traitor and was conspiring with the enemy. Why else had he sent the King to Dover? Again and again he shook his head.

"Wherefore to Dover?" repeated Regan, with fierce insistence.

"Because I would not see thy cruel nails pluck out his poor old eyes!" cried out the Earl, driven at last to pour out all the pent-up anger in his heart against Lear's monstrous children; and he prayed that he might live to see vengeance overtake them!

"See it thou never shall!" shouted the Duke and, while servants held the old Earl firmly, he reached out, and, with sharp fingers, tore out one of his eyes!

"The other, too!" urged Regan eagerly, as if the old man's shrieks and screams of agony had made her hot for more.

"Hold your hand, my Lord!" cried out a servant, scarce able to believe what his master had done. The Duke turned on him. Swords were out. They fought. The servant wounded his master; then paid for his brave humanity by losing it. Regan stabbed him from behind.

"My Lord," breathed the dying man to Gloucester, "you have one eye left to see some mischief on him . . ." But the Duke, scowling heavily from his wound, shook his head. "Out, vile jelly!" he panted, and, with red nails, clawed out the other eye.

Gloucester was in darkness and unimagined pain. "Where is my son Edmund?" he moaned. Only to be told that it was Edmund who had betrayed him to the monsters in the castle. Then he knew what eyes had never let him see: that he, like the old King, had cast out the true child and had cherished the worst.

"Go thrust him out at gates," ordered Regan contemptuously, "and let him smell his way to Dover."

He was led away; and servants, out of sight of their

mistress and master, soothed his bleeding face with whites of eggs, and gently bandaged over his horrible lack of eyes. It was morning when he stumbled out of the castle gates, though night to him. Everywhere, broken trees, weeping hedgerows and ruined fields bore witness to the fury that had been outside; the old Earl, with two red flowers for eyes, bore witness to the savagery that had been within.

An ancient countryman, a tenant of the Earl's, saw him fumbling the air, and was at once filled with pity. He took him by the hand and led him away from the castle. Gloucester begged him to go away, for he feared that any who helped him would suffer for it, even as he had suffered for helping the King.

"You cannot see your way," answered the ancient one, as if that was reason enough for setting pity above common sense. So they wandered on, the tenant carefully keeping his blind lord out of the ditches that ran, like silver sores, along the sides of the road.

Edgar was on that road, and he saw the old countryman leading his father. Then he saw his father's eyeless face, and horror seized him, and wild disbelief!

"'Tis poor mad Tom," said the countryman, recognizing the naked madman who stood, staring and trembling in their way.

"Is that the naked fellow?" asked Gloucester, remembering the King's strange companion in the storm; and when he heard that it was indeed the same fellow, he asked poor Tom to lead him to Dover. But first he begged the countryman to fetch some clothing for his naked guide.

"I'll bring the best 'parel that I have!" promised the old fellow, and hastened away to his poor cottage, as if it was a treasure-house, overflowing with plenty. While they waited, Gloucester told his guide of a certain cliff near to Dover, that reared high above the sea. It was to the top of this cliff that he wished to be taken; for it was in his mind to end his miseries by plunging from that place.

"Give me thy arm," answered Edgar, in poor Tom's voice, for he dared not trust his own. "Poor Tom shall lead thee."

Serpents do not sicken from their own venom, but men do. Already Lear's evil daughters and Gloucester's evil son were being poisoned by the very instruments that had brought them power: greed, lust, cruelty, envy and ambition. The Duke of Cornwall was dead; he had died of the wound given him by his servant. Regan, his widow, lusted for Edmund, the handsome new Earl of Gloucester; so also did her sister Goneril, Duchess of Albany, who loathed and despised her own husband, whose mild nature shrank from his wife's merciless strength. The two sisters hated each other; and Edmund, smiling, clever Edmund, who had sworn undying affection to both of them, cared not which murdered the other for love of him, for he loved himself far better.

The Duke of Albany, a weak but honourable man, who had grieved for what had become of the King, rejoiced when he learned that the Duke of Cornwall had perished for his monstrous cruelty to Gloucester; and it was only because of the threat to the kingdom itself that he joined forces with Regan and Edmund, and marched upon Dover.

The land trembled under the tread of bony soldiers and gaunt horses; and the banners of Albany, Cornwall and Gloucester streamed out over the two Duchesses, who rode more murderously against each other, than against the invading French. Edmund rode with Regan, who, being widowed, had the better claim; so Goneril sent Oswald, her steward, with a letter to Edmund, begging him to murder the Duke of Albany: then she would be a widow, too.

But when Oswald arrived, Edmund had gone. He had ridden on ahead to seek out his father and kill him, before his wretched state moved too many to anger against those who had brought him to it.

"What might import my sister's letter?" asked Regan, staring at the sealed paper and consumed with jealous suspicions.

"I know not, my Lady," answered the steward.

She did not believe him. "I'll love thee much," she offered coaxingly. "Let me unseal the letter."

But Oswald was faithful; so Regan was forced to content herself with hiding her anger and telling the steward to warn his mistress that Edmund was not for her. Then, as Oswald rode on after Edmund, Regan called out, as a bloody afterthought, that he would be well rewarded if he found the blind Earl of Gloucester and killed him.

The blind old Earl, his wounds congealed to two black clusters, wandered in a field not far from Dover. Edgar, still unknown, led him by the hand.

"When shall I come to the top of that same hill?" he asked, wearily.

"You do climb up it now," answered Edgar.

"Methinks the ground is even," said the blind man.

"Horrible steep," promised Edgar, and, with breaking heart, persuaded his father that he stood at the very summit of a cliff so high that it made the brain sway to look down.

The blind man knelt and, giving all he had of value to his guide, took his last farewell of the world. Then he leaped, and fell, foolishly, face forward on the ground.

Edgar ran towards him, and, in a changed voice but still not his own, exclaimed in wonderment that the blind man had not been dashed to pieces! that he was unharmed! that it was not to be believed that he had fallen so far and dropped as gently as a feather! "Thy life's a miracle!" he declared; and prayed that the great shock his father had sustained would bring him out of the utter darkness of the spirit. He could not endure for his father to die in despair. Anxiously he watched the blind face turn from side to side, watching its looks change, until at last disbelief and misery softened . . .

"Henceforth," sighed Gloucester, "I'll bear affliction . . ."

"Bear free and patient thoughts," murmured Edgar, gently raising his father. "But who comes here?"

A strange fantastic figure was wandering through the high-grown corn; a mad, wild old man, stuck all over with wild flowers, and crowned with weeds. It was King Lear. He had escaped from his attendants, who, even now, were searching for him to bring him to Cordelia.

"No, they cannot touch me for coining," he announced weirdly. "I am the King himself."

"I know that voice!" cried Gloucester.

"Ha! Goneril with a white beard!" said the King, as if Gloucester's horrible eyes reminded him of his daughter's. Then he talked reproachfully about the world, which he no longer liked; and the wind and the rain which had made him unhappy and given him pains in his bones, even though people had told him he was the King. Then he recognized Gloucester and jeered at his lost sight. Then he strayed to talking about men and women, all of whom filled him with disgust. He shuddered and shut his eyes. They were all liars, cheats, lechers and thieves, with nothing but lies to choose between them. Then his frantic mind, which had buzzed like a wasp over all the wide universe, came back to his children. His eyes blazed. "Kill, kill, kill, kill, kill, kill!" he screamed; and began to run away, for he had seen his attendants coming for him.

This way and that way he capered, to avoid outstretched arms. "Come and you get it!" he shouted. "You shall get it by running! Sa, sa, sa, sa!" And away he went, weeds and flowers falling from him everywhere, and his attendants running after.

Briefly a gentleman stayed to talk with Edgar of the poor King's state, and of Cordelia, the daughter who truly loved him. The French army had moved on, to do battle with the advancing British, but she was waiting for her father.

"How near's the other army?" asked Edgar, anxious for his own father's safety.

"Near, and on speedy foot," answered the gentleman. Edgar thanked him, and, when he had gone, began to lead his father away.

There was a horseman galloping along the road, a dainty horseman with plumes in his hat and a letter tucked importantly in his belt. Seeing the blind man, he reined in and dismounted. "A proclaimed prize!" he cried, his eyes bright with thoughts of advancement. "Most happy!" It was Oswald, and he drew his sword to kill the blind traitor. But Edgar opposed him. "Out, dunghill!" Oswald shouted, struggling fiercely; but the dunghill proved the better man, and Oswald fell, dying, to the ground. With his last breath he begged Edgar to bury his body and not leave it to rot in the air, and to take the letter he carried to Edmund, Earl of Gloucester. Then he died.

Edgar took the letter, and opened it. As he read it his hand trembled and his face grew pale, for the villainy in Goneril's letter to his brother showed him a world more monstrous than ever he could have imagined. As he crouched, wondering what he should do, he heard the sound of distant drums.

The running King had been caught. Gentle hands had taken him, and tended him, and washed him, and put him in fine soft clothes.

"How does my royal Lord? How fares Your Majesty?" asked a low, soft voice he thought he knew; and above him, with smiling lips and eyes bright with tears, was a countenance he remembered as from an old dream.

"Sir, do you know me?" asked the lady.

He pondered the matter deeply, then answered as truthfully as he could: "Pray do not mock me: I am a very foolish, fond old man ... and to deal plainly, I fear I am not in my perfect mind. Methinks I should know you and know this man."

The Earl of Kent, who was standing beside Cordelia, bowed his head as his heart broke.

"Do not laugh at me," said the King anxiously, "for as I am a man, I think this lady to be my child Cordelia."

"And so I am, I am!" wept Cordelia; and King Lear's darkness lifted, and the world shone, as he embraced the child he had banished from his favour, but never from his heart.

The Duke of Albany, mild and courteous even in steel, had been given a letter. He and his Duchess, together with Regan and Edmund, had been walking among the iron forest of their joined forces, pausing here and there to talk with captains, and to glance along the corpse-faces of their soldiers, when a roughly dressed fellow, his face half hidden under a peasant's hood, beckoned to him. He stepped aside, leaving his wife and her sister, with Edmund between them, to walk on. Then the fellow had thrust a paper into his hand, begging him to read it before the battle, and alone. The Duke had asked him to wait, but he would not. He had hastened away, saying that he would return when a herald's trumpet should sound for a champion to come forward and answer for what the letter contained. When the fellow had gone, the Duke read the letter. His hand shook and his face grew pale, even as

Edgar's had done. It was his wife's letter to Edmund, contriving his own murder. Edgar had given it to him. The Duke put the letter away and rejoined Edmund and the two sisters. He said nothing, for the battle drums had begun to roll and thunder.

With heavy tread, the two armies began to move against each other, at first slowly and then with increasing speed, until, with tremendous clanking and loud shouts, they met. Gaunt-eyed men fought gaunt-eyed men, struggling to and fro over the harmless land. It was a world more to die in than to live in, as crops were destroyed, cottages shattered, and men and horses screamed where birds had sung. Soon the field was a graveyard: some had died bravely, some in flight, but it made no difference as they lay, making poppies with their blood.

The French were defeated and among the prisoners were King Lear and Cordelia, who, though she might have escaped, would not leave her father's side. Edmund's men had captured them.

"Take them away," said Edmund curtly. He did not hate them, but they were in his way; and he was never so foolish as to put pity before gain.

"Come, let's away to prison," said King Lear, with his arm proudly about his daughter's shoulders, "we two alone will sing like birds i' the cage . . ." What he had lost in freedom, he had gained in love.

When the old man and his child had been led away, Edmund sent a captain after them, to kill them both.

No sooner had the officer gone, than the Duke of Albany, with Goneril and Regan, came to greet Edmund and praise him for the courage he had shown in the battle. The sisters were extravagant in their admiration; but the Duke was somewhat cooler. As Edmund swelled in importance under the glowing looks of the ladies, the Duke said coldly: "I hold you but as a subject of this war, not as a brother."

Angrily Edmund began to assert himself, when the Duke raised his hand. "Edmund," he said, "I arrest thee on capital treason; and – " (here he pointed to his wife) "this gilded serpent."

He said nothing of the letter. The time for that would come; and soon. Even he, mild Albany, had reached his limit of enduring creatures so devilish: the evil young Earl, the vile Regan, and, worst of all, the monster who was his wife.

Loudly Edmund was demanding that any man who dared to call him a traitor should come forward and prove the charge in single combat; any man, even the Duke himself. Goneril was smiling, and Albany knew that she longed for him to take up the challenge, for Edmund, fiercely confident Edmund, would have killed him in moments. Nonetheless, he was resolved.

Suddenly he saw that Regan was distressed. Her face was white and crumpled with pain. "She is not well," he said abruptly, "convey her to my tent." When the trembling Duchess had been helped away, he called a herald. "Let the trumpet sound!" he commanded. Edmund looked at him almost pityingly, and Goneril's smile broadened. If no man came forward at the trumpet's third blast, then he himself would have to fight. Already the wicked pair saw him dead. Even so, thought Albany, as the trumpet sounded, it would be better than living in their world.

Then, at the third blast, a man in armour appeared. The stranger had kept his word. He wore a helmet with the visor down. Who was he? He would say no more than that he was of noble birth, and equal with the man he challenged.

Edmund was no coward, and, though he would sooner have killed the Duke, he accepted the unknown challenger. The trumpet sounded again, and all stood back as the two men drew their swords and began to fight. Albany saw his wife's eyes glitter as she watched

22

her lover and prayed for him. He saw her lips part with joy as Edmund seemed to have the upper hand; then he saw her grow pale with fear, and her hand fly to her mouth to stifle a cry of dismay, as Edmund fell. He had been pierced through the side by the stranger's sword! Savagely she cried out that the contest had been unjust, that Edmund had been tricked.

"Shut your mouth, dame!" commanded her husband; and he held up the letter! She stared at it, her face grey with dread. She tried to seize the letter. He thrust her away. "No tearing, lady," he warned. "I perceive you know it."

"Ask me not what I know!" she shouted; and rushed frantically away.

Edmund was dying. He lay where he had fallen and his conqueror knelt beside him. He had confessed to his crimes, and now wanted only to know whose hand had killed him. Edgar took off his helmet. Edmund gazed up at the brother he had betrayed, and sighed: "The wheel is come full circle . . ."

Then, for Edmund's life was ebbing fast, Edgar told him of their father and of how he had guided and supported the blind old man and had brought him to some sort of peace before he had died. The old Earl of Gloucester was dead. But he had not died in despair. At the very last he had learned who his guide had been. Joy had transfigured his ruined face. His heart had leaped – and then, said Edgar gently, "burst smilingly."

Edmund nodded; his brother's words had moved him deeply, perhaps, even, to do some good before it was too late. But suddenly there was a cry of, "Help, help! O help!" and a man came running, his face fearful and with a bloody knife in his hand! Goneril had killed herself; and Regan also lay dead. She had been poisoned by her sister for love of Edmund, if ever it

23

could have been love that had inhabited that pitiless heart. The monsters had destroyed each other.

"I was contracted to them both; all three now marry in an instant," murmured Edmund, without regret. Then he remembered the good he had wished to do and, with his dying breath, begged that a messenger should go to the prison and save Cordelia and the King. He sent his sword with the messenger, so that the man should be believed.

But it was too late. There came a cry, a dreadful, desolate cry, that seemed to fill the world with its ancient misery. "Howl, howl, howl, howl!" wailed King Lear, as he stumbled over the rough ground with Cordelia, dead in his arms. He stopped and stared at those who watched him, with grief and horror in their eyes.

"A plague upon you, murderers, traitors all! I might have saved her . . ." And then, looking down on the dead face, said proudly: "I killed the slave that was a-hanging thee."

Then he seemed to forget his terrible burden, for he peered at Albany, at Edgar, and then at Kent, who had followed him through his darkest days, and now stood helpless at journey's end. He shook his head, and looked again.

"Who are you? Mine eyes are not o' the best: I'll tell you straight." He frowned. "Are you not Kent?" He nodded. "You are welcome hither," he said, as he saw, in the banished Earl, the faithful servant whose love and care had watched over him.

Then he sank to the ground, as if the small weight he carried in his arms was a world in heaviness. "And my poor fool is hanged!" he sighed, no longer knowing which child was which, Cordelia or his Fool, for both were dead. "Thou'lt come no more, never, never, never, never, never! I pray you, undo this button," he begged, as all his power and all his royal greatness dwindled down to this one last little need. "Thank you, sir . . ." Then his eyes brightened as he fancied, for a moment, that Cordelia still lived. "Look there, look there!" he cried; and then no more.

"Look up, my Lord!" cried Edgar.

"Vex not his ghost," said Kent. "O let him pass. He hates him that would upon the rack of this tough world stretch him out longer."

King Lear was dead.

Hamlet

It happened in Denmark, long ago. High up on the battlements of the castle at Elsinore, two sentinels, their cloaks snapping in the whipping dark, met at the limit of their watch: the one ending, the other beginning. Their faces, seen faintly by the light of a thin seeding of stars, were white as bone. It was midnight. Presently they were joined by two companions, and the relieved sentinel took his departure, very gladly. The three remaining stared uneasily about them.

"What, has this thing appeared again tonight?" asked one of the newcomers, a young man by name of Horatio.

"I have seen nothing," answered the sentinel, but softly and with many a wary look about him.

For two nights now the sentinels had seen a strange, unnatural sight. Between midnight and one o'clock, a phantom figure had soundlessly stalked the battlements. It had been, so far as could be made out in the shaking dark, the spirit of the dead King.

"Tush, tush, 'twill not appear," murmured Horatio. He was a visitor to Elsinore from Wittenburg, where he had been at the University with Prince Hamlet, the dead King's son. Being a student of philosophy and not much given to dreaming, he had little faith in ghosts, phantoms and spectres of the night. He smiled at his pale companions, who had dragged him up to this cold, dark, windy place with their fantastic tale of –

"Look where it comes again!"

He looked; and his sensible eyes started from his sensible head. All reason fled for in weirdly gleaming armour and with weightless tread, the dead King stalked slowly by! The watchers, huddled in their cloaks, trembled with amazement and dread.

"Speak to it, Horatio!" breathed one, for the apparition seemed to linger. Horatio made the attempt, as boldly as he was able; and the night seemed to freeze as the dead King turned upon them a shadowy countenance that was grim with grief. Then it stalked away, and vanished into some invisible curtain of the night.

They watched after it till their eyes ached with staring; then they turned to one another in bewilderment. What could be the meaning of the apparition? Why had the dead King returned, and with looks so heavy with despair? Horatio, a little recovered in voice and colour, supposed the cause to lie in some danger to the state. Fortinbras, the Prince of Norway, was arming to seize back the lands that the dead King had boldly conquered. Surely it was this threat that had troubled the King's spirit and had dragged it from the grave?

But even as he proposed such a cause, which seemed likely enough, the ghost returned, as if to deny it.

"Stay!" cried Horatio, "if thou hast any sound or use of voice, speak to me!"

But it would not. It raised its arms as if in horror. From far off, a cock crew. The phantom wavered, became insubstantial, then faded, leaving on the dark air no more than an impress of measureless grief and despair.

"It was about to speak when the cock crew," whispered one.

"And then it started like a guilty thing upon a fearful summons," said Horatio; and straightway it was agreed that Prince Hamlet should be told of what had been seen. If to no one else, the dead father would surely speak to his living son.

The King, the great, good King, loved and honoured by all, had been dead for two months. He had been stung by a serpent while sleeping in his orchard, and all Denmark had wept. But now the time for grieving was past: sad eyes gave way to merry ones, long faces to round smiles; and the heavy black of mourning, that had bandaged up the court, was washed away by a sea of bright colour. Yellow silks and sky-blue satins, encrusted with silver, blazed in the ceremonial chamber, and the walls were hung with glory. There was a new King – even though there was still the same Queen. She had married again, and with her dead husband's brother.

This new King was a sturdy gentleman, broad-shouldered and broad-featured, and much given to smiling – as well he might, for he had gained a luxurious throne and a luxurious queen at a stroke. Affably he conducted the affairs of state, dispatching ambassadors to Norway to patch up grievances and giving gracious permission to Laertes, his faithful chamberlain's son, to return to France whence he'd come to attend the coronation. Next, still smiling, and with his strong hand guarding the jewelled hand of his Queen, he turned to her son, Prince Hamlet, a young man in black, like a plain thought in a gaudy world.

"But now, my cousin Hamlet, and my son – "

"A little more than kin, and less than kind," murmured the Prince, with a look of dislike and contempt.

Anxiously the Queen, his mother, begged him to forsake his dark looks and dark attire. He answered her with scarcely more courtesy than he had shown the King. The King, hiding his annoyance, added his own urgings; and the young man submitted – to the extent of agreeing to remain at court and not return to school at Wittenberg as he had wished. The King was satisfied and, with more smiles (which he dispensed like the small coin of royal charity), he left the chamber with the backward-glancing Queen upon his arm. As if on apron-strings, the crowding courtiers followed.

Hamlet was alone. Long and hard he stared after the departed court. The look upon his face, had it been seen by the royal pair who had inspired it, would have chilled their hearts, made stone of their smiles, and poison of the lust of their bed. Dull hatred oppressed the young man's mind: hatred for the corrupted world in which he was imprisoned, hatred for life itself, and loathing and disgust for the Queen, his mother, who, so soon after her noble husband's death, had married so wretched a creature as the dead King's brother.

"O most wicked speed!" he cried out in anguish, as, helplessly, his imagination both probed and shrank from the hateful circumstance. "To post with such dexterity to incestuous sheets!"

But someone was coming! Hastily he hid all evidence of his breaking heart under his customary mask of indifferent courtesy.

"Hail to your lordship," a gentleman said, coming into the chamber.

"I am glad to see you well," responded Hamlet, scarcely looking up, and with the distant cousin of a smile. Then he saw that the gentleman was no tedious courtier. It was Horatio, his old school friend Horatio, from Wittenberg!

At once, surprise and delight overspread his countenance. His gloom vanished and his sunk spirit revived. In a moment he was all quickness and liveliness and eager hospitality, as he greeted his good friend from Wittenberg, where life had been clear and honest, where the plain rooms had been enriched with noble ideas, not sullen tapestries, and the talk had flowed like wine. Warmly he included in his greeting Horatio's two companions, who were soldiers of the Royal Guard. Then, turning to his friend, he inquired:

"But what is your affair in Elsinore?"

"My lord, I came to see your father's funeral."

"I prithee, do not mock me, fellow student," said Hamlet, his smile, like the sun in winter, forgetting its warmth. "I think it was to see my mother's wedding."

"Indeed, my lord," admitted Horatio, gently, "it followed hard upon."

"Thrift, thrift, Horatio. The funeral baked meats did coldly furnish forth the marriage tables," said Hamlet. Then his bitter mood lightened and his smile regained some warmth. "My father," he murmured softly, "Methinks I see my father – "

Horatio and his companions started. "Where, my lord?"

"In my mind's eye, Horatio," said Hamlet; and his listeners grew easy again.

"I saw him once," said Horatio. "'A was a goodly king."

"'A was a man," said Hamlet, as if wanting to dispense with all worldly distinction of office. "Take him for all in all: I shall not look upon his like again."

Then Horatio told him. Eagerly, and yet careful to keep within the exact observation of a scholar, he told of the appearance of the dead King upon the battlements. "I knew your father," he assured the Prince. "These hands are not more like."

Hamlet listened, with fiercely beating heart; but old Wittenberg habits of argument, question and debate made him cautious.

"Armed, say you?"

"Armed, my lord."

"From top to toe?"

"My lord, from head to foot."

"Then saw you not his face?" demanded Hamlet, triumphantly.

"O yes, my lord, he wore his beaver up."

There was no doubt. The spirit had been, to all intents, the ghost of Hamlet's father. With huge and dreadful excitement, Hamlet promised that he would join Horatio and the soldiers on the battlements on the following night.

"My father's spirit – in arms," he breathed, when he was alone. "All is not well . . ."

Laertes was for France. Handsomely dressed in the newest fashion for his journey, he came to bid farewell to his sister Ophelia and give her such advice upon the perils and pitfalls of the world as he thought to be necessary. She was young and fair and modest as a bud. She was of so yielding a nature that she dared not call her soul her own, and had put it, trustingly, in the care of her brother and her wise old father, Polonius, the chamberlain. She had confided in Laertes that Prince Hamlet had, of late, caused her to believe that he loved her; and now, as she sat in a window seat, stitching some nursery proverb into a sampler, she listened as her brother solemnly warned her of the danger of passion and the unsteady nature of a young man's love. She nodded and nodded, and, when he had finished, she looked up and expressed the timid hope that he would practise as he had preached. Indignantly he protested his own virtue, and was about to depart when his father, Polonius, appeared.

"Yet here, Laertes? Aboard, aboard for shame!" cried the old gentleman; and then, taking advantage of the moment, saw fit to advise his son, even as his son had advised his sister. But yet there was a difference; for while Laertes had warned his sister of dangers that might threaten her from without, Polonius warned of those subtler dangers from within. Although they were, for the most part, threadbare maxims such as Ophelia might have embroidered on her samplers, they were not unfitting.

"Costly thy habit as thy purse can buy," said Polonius, severely eyeing his over-dressed son, "but not expressed in fancy: rich, not gaudy . . ."

At the mention of "purse", the young man's hand had gone helplessly to his side, which caused Polonius to warn, "Neither a borrower nor a lender be . . ." The young man grew red; but, nevertheless, listened patiently until his father had done. Then, turning to his sister and reminding her of his own advice, he took his departure in a blaze of mostly good intentions.

"What is't, Ophelia, he hath said to you?" asked her father suspiciously.

Timidly Ophelia confessed that it had to do with the Lord Hamlet. The old man nodded; he had suspected as much.

"What is between you?" he demanded. "Give me up the truth."

"He hath, my lord, of late," murmured the girl, dividing her looks between her proverb and her father, "made many tenders of his affection to me."

"Affection!" exclaimed Polonius contemptuously. "Pooh, you speak like a green girl!" And then and there he berated her soundly for her foolishness in believing in a prince's love. He warned her (as her brother had done) of the danger that might lie in Hamlet's fondness – a danger not only to herself, but, more importantly, to that wily politician who was her father. Sternly he forbade her to have any further talk with Prince Hamlet; and she, mild Ophelia, who had already given up the charge of her soul, now gave up the charge of her heart. "I shall obey, my lord," she said.

* * *

The night was bitter and the frozen stars peered secretly down upon the three cloaked figures who stood upon the castle's battlements.

"What hour now?" asked Hamlet for perhaps the hundredth time.

"I think it lacks of twelve," answered Horatio.

If the dead King was to appear, his time was almost come. Suddenly there came the sound of festive trumpets and the double thunder of a cannon.

"What does this mean, my lord?" wondered Horatio.

It was a custom, expounded Hamlet, with a sour smile, for such uproarious noise to accompany the revelry and drinking of the King. It brought the nation into disrepute, and made them seem to be no more than idle drunkards, so that, whatever of good there was, was lost in bad report. From this, Hamlet's unresting mind hovered over the curious circumstances of how a single defect in a man might, in the general view, taint and discolour his fairest virtues.

"Look, my lord, it comes!" Horatio's voice was sharp with fear; his hand shook as he pointed.

Hamlet turned. His face grew pale, his eyes huge, and his expelled breath made a thread of grey amazement in the air.

"Angels and ministers of grace defend us!" he cried out.

Upon the dark battlements stood his dead father! All in armour, as cold and lifeless as himself, the dead King gazed with tragic sorrow upon his shaking son. He beckoned, and Hamlet made to follow. Urgently his companions – Horatio and the sentinel – tried to prevent him, for they dreaded that the spirit might be malevolent and would tempt the young Prince to his death. Savagely Hamlet threw off the restraint and threatened to strike with his sword if he should be hindered any more.

"Go on," he cried to the beckoning ghost, "I'll follow thee!"

The dead King stalked on and the wild Prince went after, till both were lost from sight.

"Let's follow!" urged the sentinel, fearful for his Prince.

"To what issue will this come?" whispered Horatio.

The sentinel stared into the freezing darkness in which the dead King and his son had vanished. "Something is rotten in the state of Denmark," he said.

Father and son stood close together in a secret fold of the night. The young man shuddered as the unnatural chill of his dead father struck through to his heart.

"Mark me," whispered the ghost.

"I will," breathed his son.

"My hour is almost come," sighed the spirit; and, as it told of the grim and hateful regions to which it was soon condemned to return, Hamlet stared into his father's shadowy, unhappy eyes and longed, with all his heart, to kiss his freezing hand and pour out, into his hollow ear, all the love and devotion that death had stopped.

"List, list, O list!" begged the ghost, with sudden urgency. "If thou didst ever thy dear father love – "

"O God!"

"Revenge his foul and most unnatural murder!"

"Murder!"

The stars glared, the battlements shuddered, and Hamlet's heart ceased as the terrible word was uttered. Murder! And revenge!

"Now, Hamlet, hear," whispered the ghost. "The serpent that did sting thy father's life now wears his crown!"

"O my prophetic soul! My uncle!"

Sombrely the dead man observed and approved the quickening of anger in his son, and went on to unfold the hideous circumstance of the crime, of how the King's loving wife, Hamlet's mother, had been seduced by the King's wretched brother, and then, how that brother had poured poison in the sleeping King's ear.

"Thus was I, sleeping, by a brother's hand, of life, of crown, of queen at once dispatch'd . . ."

Consumed with rage and horror, the son listened to his father's words, each one of which seemed a command for revenge upon the unwholesome pair whose faint rejoicings, from time to time, mocked the night.

"But howsomever thou pursuest this act," warned the ghost, with a sudden tenderness made horrible by its hopelessness, "taint not thy mind nor let thy soul contrive against thy mother aught. Leave her to heaven . . ."

Hamlet's heart ached with pity, for he saw that his father's spirit was tormented by love no less than by hate: both had outlived the grave. But now the night was wearing threadbare, and the phantom shivered as the dark grew thin and patched. "Fare thee well," it whispered. "Adieu, adieu, adieu. Remember me." Then it was gone and Hamlet stood alone.

Breathing harshly he leaned against the battlements and rested his head upon the cold stone, as if to support his staggering mind. Far, far below, a wild sea crashed and raged against the rocks at the base of the cliff upon which the castle stood; but darkness and disturbance reduced its fury to silent, tumbled lace. Yet had it been seen in all its huge madness, it would have seemed no more than distance had made it beside the raging in Hamlet's soul. He raised his head and, with eyes blazing with tears, swore to heaven that he would be the instrument of the ghost's revenge. He would wipe from his mind all the calmness, wisdom and fine thoughts he had learned in happy Wittenberg, and leave behind only – revenge!

"O most pernicious woman!" he wept, as again he

heard sounds of distant revelry. "O villain, villain, smiling damned villain!" With trembling hands he drew a book from his pocket – a student's book in which observations of life and nature were noted down. "Meet it is I set it down," he muttered, as if to calm his extreme agitation by such scholar's habit, "that one may smile, and smile, and be a villain." He wrote so fiercely that he scored the paper through. He put the book away. "It is 'Adieu, adieu, remember me'," he repeated. "I have sworn't!" He drew his sword as if meaning, then and there, to rush down into the black castle and kill its poisoned heart.

But he heard voices calling. His companions were searching for him. Desperately he searched for some secret place in his mind where he might hide the dreadful knowledge he possessed; he would not, he dared not, confide what the ghost had revealed. When his companions found him, and eagerly questioned him, he answered them with wild, fantastic humour which, to his great relief, bewildered them into asking no more. Nonetheless he made them swear, upon the cross of his sword, that they would never tell of what had happened that night. This they did, and more than once; for wherever they stood, Hamlet heard the ghost, deep in the earth, calling: "Swear!"

"This is wondrous strange," said Horatio, troubled by his friend's frantic manner.

"And therefore as a stranger give it welcome," returned Hamlet; and then, with a sad smile at his old school friend, said: "There are more things in heaven and earth, Horatio, than are dreamt of in your philosophy."

He made them swear again, this time that, if his mad humour should continue, they would never betray that they suspected what lay behind it. He trusted no one, least of all himself. His heart was so full that he dared not trust his tongue not to betray him. Madness would be his refuge and hiding place of truth, until the time was ripe for his revenge.

Revenge! He shrank within himself as the full horror of his circumstance came upon him. What was he, Horatio's fellow student, doing in this dark world of murder and revenge, of treacherous kings and faithless queens, of creeping courtiers and poison? Most bitterly he sighed:

"The time is out of joint. O cursed spite, that ever I was born to set it right."

Laertes was in France and out of his father's sight, but by no means out of that cautious old gentleman's mind. Polonius did not trust his son; and perhaps not without cause. He sent a servant to spy on him and on what company he kept.

Polonius, cunning old adviser to king after king, deemed it his duty to know everything. Consequently if walls had ears, they were Polonius's; if keyholes had eyes, they were likewise, Polonius's. Yet this abundance of knowledge did not make him wise; it made him merely knowing. Thus when his daughter Ophelia came to him, as she was in duty bound, and told him that the Lord Hamlet had appeared in her room while she was sewing, with the looks of a melancholy madman, he sought no further for a cause than in disappointed love. "Have you given him any hard words of late?" he asked.

"No, my good lord," she answered, with a downcast look, "but as you did command, I did repel his letters and denied his access to me."

"That hath made him mad," pronounced Polonius. "Come, go we to the King. This must be known . . ."

But Hamlet's strangeness had already troubled the smooth surface of the court, puzzled the smiling King and vaguely distressed the easy Queen. Knowing that nothing would be got from the loyal Horatio, two other school friends of Hamlet had been sent for, in the hope that they would discover the cause of the Prince's change. Rosencrantz and Guildenstern, two courtly scholars, so alike in bows and smiles and flattered pleasure at being Royally summoned, that the King was hard put to know which was Guildenstern and which was Rosencrantz. However, the two fledgling courtiers had no such difficulty in knowing the King, and divining, amid the oiled smiles that slipped from face to face, that they would be well paid for spying on their old friend and smelling out the secrets of his heart.

"Heavens make our presence and our practices pleasant and helpful to him," said Guildenstern to Hamlet's mother, judging that such tender interest would concern her more than it would the King.

But it would seem that the young men's skills were not to be needed. No sooner had the bowing pair departed, to search out Hamlet, than Polonius came bustling in, stuffed with good news. First, from Norway. Young Fortinbras asked for no more than the free passage of his army through Denmark to some distant spot. Next, and best of all, the cause of Hamlet's madness had been discovered. Polonius had found it out. What was it? The King and Queen waited while the old politician, who could never be plain, used up words like stuffing, to swell the importance of a small goose before serving it up.

"More matter with less art," said the Queen impatiently and Polonius, thus brought, unwillingly, to the point, produced a letter written by Hamlet to Ophelia. It was a love letter of the most sentimental kind.

"Came this from Hamlet to her?" wondered the Queen, as if surprised that her son could pen such poor stuff.

It had indeed.

"But how hath she received his love?" asked the King, curiously.

Polonius, uninterested in his daughter's heart, replied by explaining that he had thought it fitting to put a stop to the business. "Lord Hamlet," he had warned his daughter, "is a prince out of thy star. This must not be." Very properly he had forbidden her to speak with the Prince again. But since then he had learned of such matters from his daughter as had left him in no doubt as to what had staggered the young man's brain. Unrequited love.

"Do you think 'tis this?" asked the King of Hamlet's mother.

"It may be," sighed the Queen, over whose own heart love, passion and lust exercised a sovereign sway. "Very like."

But the King was not entirely convinced. He would like more evidence.

"How may we try it further?" he asked.

To Polonius, the ever-resourceful Polonius, this presented not the smallest difficulty. Hamlet, he recollected, was accustomed to walk in the lobby for hours at a time. "At such a time," he proposed, with the heartless eagerness of the seasoned conspirator, "I'll loose my daughter to him." What passed then between the girl and the Prince might easily be overheard from a suitable place of concealment. (Such places were, to Polonius, as familiar as his study; and, doubtless, furnished with comfortable chairs.) Readily the King fell in with the scheme, but further talk was prevented by the appearance of Hamlet himself. He was reading a book; and so deeply was he sunk in it that he might have been walking upon some lonely heath, instead of through the richly peopled rooms of the royal palace of Denmark. In appearance, Hamlet was somewhat declined. His shoes were unfastened, his stockings wrinkled, and his shirt hanging loose, like a limp surrender. Polonius nodded knowingly. He urged the King and Queen to depart and leave all to him, which they did most gladly. Hamlet seemed not to see them go.

"How does my good Lord Hamlet?" inquired Polonius, with the patient kindness that might be offered to an idiot or a child.

"Well, God a-mercy," returned the Prince, not looking up.

"Do you know me, my lord?" pursued Polonius.

The Prince looked at him carefully. "Excellent well," he said. "You are a fishmonger."

Somewhat taken aback, Polonius denied the charge, and then found himself caught in a swirling net of nonsense, of daughters, maggots and graves, from which he was glad to escape, when Rosencrantz and Guildenstern, out of breath from searching, at last found their friend.

"My excellent good friends!" cried Hamlet, throwing off all his madness and most of his melancholy in a moment. "Good lads, how do you both?"

They laughed, and he laughed; and, for a little while, they were no more than three good friends delighting in each other's shrewd wit and wisdom; and, for a little while, the grim horror and despair of Hamlet's situation seemed to him to be no more than an evil dream . . . until, in all innocence and courtesy, he asked:

"But in the beaten way of friendship, what make you at Elsinore?"

"To visit you, my lord," they answered promptly, "no other occasion."

A little too prompt; and accompanied by looks that were a little too innocent. In moments, they who had been commissioned to worm out Hamlet's secret, had their own uncovered before they had so much as begun. They were forced to admit that they had been sent for by the Queen and King; and it needed no great skill on Hamlet's part to guess the reason. Bitterly he stared at them and reflected on how easily they had been corrupted by the poisoned world of the court. Anxiously they tried to make amends and lift the Prince's spirits. They told him that they had passed on their way to the castle a company of actors who were coming to perform before the court. It was, it seemed, a company from the city that the Prince knew well.

In spite of himself, the Prince smiled. He delighted in the play and the company of players, those excellent fellow creatures whose highest aim was to please, seemed to him the best in the world. He looked forward keenly to their arrival; but then, remembering the two pupil-spies who stood anxiously by him, he felt a pang of pity. "You are welcome," he said. "But my uncle-father and my aunt-mother are deceived."

"In what, my dear lord?" asked Guildenstern, hopefully.

"I am but mad north-north-west," said Hamlet seriously. "When the wind is southerly, I know a hawk from a handsaw."

Before they could unravel Hamlet's meaning – if, indeed, there was any – Polonius entered with the news that the players had arrived.

"The best actors in the world," read out Polonius, from the company's extensive advertisement, which reached down, like a paper apron, almost to his knees, "either for tragedy, comedy, history, pastoral, pastoral-comical, historical-pastoral, tragical-historical, tragical-comical-historical-pastoral . . ." he drew breath and read on, until the players themselves appeared.

They came into the grand ceremonial chamber where real kings and real queens and real princes held sway, and were not in the least abashed. They wore their paper crowns, clutched their wooden swords, and shrugged their patchwork gowns with a dusty dignity and a seasoning of pride.

41

"You are welcome, masters!" cried Hamlet, and shook them all warmly by the hand. He looked fondly into each well-remembered face, commented ruefully upon the damage done by years, then begged the chief actor to recite, then and there, a certain speech for which he had a particular affection.

The actor, a grand figure of a man, with the nose and eye of a battered eagle, recollected the speech and straightway launched it, as gloriously as a galleon, its sails full of wind. Either by chance, or design, the speech was from a tale of old Troy, and was full of murdered kings, revenge and mourning queens. Absorbed, Hamlet listened.

"Look," exclaimed Polonius admiringly, when the actor paused, "whe'er he has not turned his colour and has tears in's eyes. Prithee no more."

The players, pleased with the reception of this modest sample of their art, were preparing to be bustled away by Polonius to their quarters, when Hamlet detained their principal.

"Can you play 'The Murder of Gonzago'?" he asked quietly, for a curious idea was fermenting in his mind. The actor nodded. "We'll ha't tomorrow night," murmured Hamlet. "You could for a need study a speech of some dozen or sixteen lines, which I would set down and insert in't, could you not?"

The player, familiar with the vanity of poet-princes, agreed; then followed the busy chamberlain. Rosencrantz and Guildenstern likewise, bowed themselves away, doubtless to report to the King. Only Hamlet remained.

The Greek Prince, of whom the player had so roaringly told, had killed a king as bloodily quick as sword could strike; but the damned King of Denmark still lived. The Trojan Queen had rent her garments and shrieked aloud to heaven when she had seen her husband dead; but the Queen of Denmark still sighed and smiled in the bed of her husband's murderer. The player who had presented the scene had wept real tears over those long-dead griefs; the Prince of Denmark, with father murdered, mother lost to shame, and himself urged, by his father's ghost, to revenge, did nothing. "Bloody, bawdy villain!" he cried out, as his uncle's smiling face forced itself before his mind's eye. "Remorseless, treacherous, lecherous, kindless villain!" He stormed and waved his arms, even as the player had done; then shook his head. Ranting words were not to the purpose. Better think carefully of the speech he would write for tomorrow night's play. He nodded grimly. It was in his mind that the speech and the play together would represent, as nearly as was possible, the exact circumstance of his father's murder. His uncle, watching it, could not fail to be struck to the soul, and betray his guilt to the world. That is, if he *was* guilty. Hamlet frowned. Though the ghost's accusation had been, at the time, terrible in its certainty, now, in the light of a later day, it seemed remote, doubtful, and even fantastic. "I'll have grounds more relative than this," decided the undecided Prince. "The play's the thing, wherein I'll catch the conscience of the King!"

Ophelia, in her best and most delicate attire, sweetly perfumed and with sufficient red in her cheeks to sharpen her natural modesty, waited meekly while her father, closely huddled with the King and Queen, and Rosencrantz and Guildenstern, murmured about the Lord Hamlet. They were gathered in the lobby where, daily, Hamlet walked; and where she, as her father had expressed it, was to be loosed to the Prince. Presently the two young men took their bowing departures, and the Queen, after speaking kindly to Ophelia, also went away.

"Ophelia, walk you here," said her father, taking her

firmly by the arm and examining her critically as if to see if anything further might be done by way of improvement. He was anxious to be proven right in his judgement that the Prince's madness had been brought on by love for his daughter. He pressed a book into her hands and bade her read it so that her solitary walking should seem plausible. Then he and the King secreted themselves in a curtained alcove that might have been expressly made to hide such a King and such an adviser. The girl looked unhappily towards the curtain. Angrily Polonius gestured her away. The Prince was approaching. Ophelia, divided between obedience to her father, and shame for the part she had been told to play, opened her book, and shrank into the furthest obscurity she could find.

The Prince also was reading; but there was a deeper likeness between Hamlet and Ophelia than such outward show. Each had been commanded by a father, one living, one dead, to play a part for which nature had not fashioned them: Ophelia for deceit, and Hamlet for murderous revenge. In order to overcome his nature and keep his anger hot, he had returned to the book in which he had so fiercely scored his fury while the ghost's words still sounded in his ears and tore at his heart. But no such tempest tossed him now.

"To be, or not to be, that is the question:" he mused; for he had, in turning the pages, come upon the notes he had made of a great debate at Wittenberg, in which the old question had been closely argued, of whether it was better to live or to die. The arguments were strong upon both sides. Indeed, for a time, it seemed that he who argued for death had the stronger case, as he piled up, in a grim edifice, all the agonies of living that might, by the single stroke of death, be utterly demolished. And yet, as his opponent shrewdly pointed out, the death-lover, in spite of all his excellent reasons, still lived. Why did he shrink from the one act that would, by his own admission end his sufferings? The answer, as Hamlet gave it murmured utterance, was as sombre as the question. "The dread of something after death, the undiscovered country, from whose bourn no traveller returns, puzzles the will, and makes us rather bear those ills we have than fly to others that we know not of."

He shut the book and helplessly considered how closely the swaying of the argument reflected the swaying of his mind. He longed for death, which would have absolved him from the hideous duty that had been laid upon him; but he dared not rush into it. Self-murder was as repugnant to him as the murder of another. "Thus conscience doth make cowards of us all," he sighed bitterly, "and thus the native hue of resolution is sicklied o'er with the pale cast of thought . . ."

A flicker of silk and the movement of a pale hand caught the corner of his eye. He looked round and saw Ophelia. Gently she greeted him. Gently he responded. Timidly she approached him and held out a little box of trinkets he had given her. She wanted to return them. He denied all knowledge of them. Bewildered, she protested; and then came out with such a sentiment as might well have been stitched on one of her samplers: "For to the noble mind rich gifts wax poor when givers prove unkind."

Hamlet laughed, somewhat harshly. He did indeed love Ophelia, but for her dear soul and not for her unformed mind. In her stiff words he smelt out the instruction of her pompous meddling father; and he became very angry. Even she, even the lovely, simple Ophelia, was being poisoned by the general poison of the court. Savagely he turned upon her and lacerated her with the insensate fury of his tongue – even though he knew full well that no fault attached to her. But he

45

knew that whatever he said would pass directly to her father, who was an ever-open channel to the King.

"I did love you once," he said abruptly.

"Indeed, my lord, you made me believe so," faltered the girl.

"You should not have believed me," dismissed the Prince, hiding his pain under contempt. "I loved you not."

"I was the more deceived," whispered Ophelia, not knowing whether she was on her head or heels.

"Get thee to a nunnery!" shouted Hamlet wildly. Yet at the same time, he ached with pity and remorse for the frightened girl. But Ophelia could never walk the bloody path of revenge to which he was condemned. He wished only for her to escape from the foul corruption of Elsinore. "Where's your father?" he demanded suddenly.

"At home, my lord," lied Ophelia, horribly confused. And yet it was no lie she told, for Polonius's home was wherever he might hide and overhear. Nonetheless she grew pale, fearing that Hamlet had spied her father spying.

"I have heard of your paintings well enough," jeered Hamlet, seeing false colour, like treacherous flags, thrown up in her vacant cheeks. "God hath given you one face and you make yourselves another . . . Go to, I'll no more on't, it hath made me mad. I say we will have no more marriage. Those that are married already – all but one – shall live. The rest shall keep as they are. To a nunnery, go!"

With that, the mad Prince fled, leaving the girl he loved amazed and weeping on her knees. A moment later, the King and Polonius crept out of their concealment.

"Love?" said the King, his broad face bereft of smiles. "His affections do not that way tend, nor what he spake, though it lacked form a little, was not like madness. There's something in his soul . . ."

Polonius agreed, for he was not the man to disagree with his king; but he still maintained that neglected love had been the cause. "How, now, Ophelia?" he said impatiently, as his daughter's sobbing distracted him. "You need not tell us what Lord Hamlet said, we heard it all." Then, continuing to the King, proposed that the Queen might be better able to worm out her son's secret. If such a circumstance could be arranged, he, Polonius, (needless to say), would be concealed and hear all.

"It shall be so," nodded the King. "Madness in great ones must not unwatched go."

Hamlet, his face pale and his eyes glittering with excitement, waited in the great hall where the play was to be performed. Horatio was with him. Horatio knew all. Together they were to watch the King to see if he betrayed his guilt as the play unfolded the crime.

"They are coming to the play!" cried Hamlet, as the customary trumpets and drums sounded the approach of the King. "I must be idle. Get you a place!"

There was a buzzing and murmuring and laughing, and rustling and shuffling, as the King and Queen and courtly audience came in and flowed, like a silken sea, over the gilded chairs and stools and cushions that had been made ready.

"Come hither, my dear Hamlet," invited the Queen, a treasure store of pearls and diamonds and brilliant smiles, "sit by me."

Curtly the Prince declined. He took his place by Ophelia, whose brightest jewels were her eyes. But his preference seemed more spiteful than fond. He taunted her with lewd remarks that made her blush with misery, until the players' trumpet sounded the beginning of the play. The audience grew quiet, leaned forward, and misted over into a single monster of many mouths and eyes. All watched the stage – save Hamlet and Horatio, who watched the King.

At first, there was a dumb show. Gaudy painted figures stalked stiffly to and fro, and enacted, word-lessly, what might, or might not have been, the tale of a royal poisoning. The Player King grimaced, clutched air, and perished in dire agony. The King of Denmark's smile seemed nailed to his face. The dumb show ended to applause like a thin shower of hail. The dead king revived, bowed, and begged all to attend to what should follow.

"Is this a prologue, or the posy of a ring?" demanded Hamlet, consumed with impatience.

"'Tis brief, my lord," murmured Ophelia.

"As woman's love," said Hamlet, with a sharp, accus-ing look at the Queen.

Now the play began in earnest; and, though the king wore a tinsel crown, and the queen was no better than a padded boy, they spoke their love so eloquently that the Queen of Denmark sighed. But the King of Den-mark's smile still seemed nailed to his face.

"Madam how like you this play?" asked Hamlet.

"Have you heard the argument?" demanded the King. "Is there no offence in't?"

"No, no, they do but jest – poison in jest. No offence i' the world."

"What do you call the play?"

"The Mousetrap."

The play continued. The Player King lay sleeping on the boards. A murderer entered. "Thoughts black, hands apt, drugs fit, and time agreeing," he hissed; and crept towards the sleeper with black cloak trail-ing, like some malignant bat. He drew out a phial, unstoppered it and, with horrid smile, poured its deadly contents into his victim's ear. The King of Denmark's smile was gone!

"A poisons him i' the garden for his estate!" cried Hamlet, unable to contain his fierce joy. "The story is extant and written in very choice Italian. You shall see anon how the murderer gets the love of Gonzago's wife – "

The King of Denmark stood up. His eyes were blazing with anger. His face was grey with guilt.

"Give o'er the play!" cried Polonius, urgently.

"Give me some light!" shouted the enraged King. "Away!"

The play was cut off, ended before its ending. The audience had gone. Tumbled stools and chairs bore testimony to the haste of the departure. The bewildered Player King crept back to recover his tinsel crown. Then he went away, sadly shaking his head. The performance had not gone well.

But to Hamlet and Horatio the play had succeeded beyond all expectation. The King was guilty; the ghost had been honest. A furious excitement filled the Prince. He had at last set events into motion. Action had begun! His mood found expression in wild laughter and wild words, as if he had drunk strong wine. Rosencrantz and Guildenstern, pale with uneasiness, came to tell him that the King's rage had worsened. Hamlet was not distressed. The Queen, also, was much agitated.

"She desires to speak with you in her closet before you go to bed," said Rosencrantz, reproachfully.

"We shall obey," announced Hamlet, "were she ten times our mother."

Now came Polonius, limp with concern, and with the self-same message from the Queen. She would speak with her son.

The King was with Rosencrantz and Guildenstern. Breathing heavily, for his anger had by no means subsided, he confided that he thought it dangerous for the Queen's mad son to remain in court. God knew what he might do next. He must be sent away. Rosencrantz and Guildenstern, being the Prince's trusted friends (the trusted friends bowed), must accompany him to England. And without delay. No sooner had the two pupil-spies left the King, than the master-spy joined him. Polonius. His news was that Hamlet, even now, was on his way to his mother. He, Polonius, would hide and overhear whatever passed between them. The old eavesdropper hastened away, and the King, from force of habit, smiled. But it was a smile that died almost as soon as it had been born.

"O my offence is rank," he cried out in wretchedness. "It smells to heaven."

The play, with its presentation of the murder, had opened up his soul and exposed the breeding poison in it. He had murdered his brother and stolen his brother's wife. He was in agony for what he had done; and a double agony, for, though he bitterly repented his deed, he could not repent the possession of the gains it had brought him. "Help, angels!" he groaned, and knelt to pray forgiveness from God.

So deeply was he lost in his despairing plea to heaven that he never heard the soft footfall behind him, nor the sharp indrawn breath. Hamlet stood behind him, with sword upraised. He had, in passing, glimpsed the kneeling King. At once the rich, broad back invited him to the hideous duty he knew he must perform. He hesitated.

"Now might I do it," he breathed. The sword remained unmoving. The man was praying. To kill him now would send his soul to heaven. Better wait for a worse time; then he would go to hell. Silently the Prince withdrew and went upon his way.

"My words fly up," sighed the King, rising to his feet,

"my thoughts remain below. Words without thoughts never to heaven go."

Hamlet, in obedience to her wishes, came to the Queen, his mother. His mood was black with self-contempt. He had failed. Revenge had been within his grasp, and his sword had stuck in the air. It had not been because the King was at his prayers that the avenger had spared him, but because the avenger was not, by nature, an avenger. As always, thought had come between Hamlet and the deed. The consequences, like the long shadow of action, ever cooled him as he drew close. Action must needs be hot . . .

The Queen was in her bedchamber. Her hair was loose and streaked with silver, as if she had been too long in the moon. Beside her yawned the royal bed, gorged with kissing pillows and silken sheets.

"Now, mother, what's the matter?" demanded Hamlet harshly, as the rage against himself turned against the hateful scene before him.

Sharply, she reproached him. More sharply he reproached her.

"Come, come, you answer with an idle tongue," cried the Queen, with the authority of an outraged mother.

"Go, go, you question with a wicked tongue," returned Hamlet, with the authority of an outraged son. His words grew savage, violent; his look was wild, his sword was in his hand. Alarm seized the Queen. She tried to leave. Hamlet gripped her arm and forced her to sit upon the bed.

"What wilt thou do?" she shrieked in terror. "Thou wilt not murder me? Help, ho!"

"What ho! Help!" A voice, shrill with alarm, cried out from behind a curtain.

"A rat!" shouted Hamlet, whirling round in amazed fury. "Dead for a ducat, dead!"

He plunged his sword deep into the curtain. He felt

it enter more than cloth and air. He heard the sighing cry of a life escaping!

"What hast thou done?" cried out the Queen in dread.

"Nay, I know not," whispered Hamlet, staring at his dripping blade. He trembled with excitement. "Is it the King?"

He drew back the curtain. Polonius glared up at him. He had killed the eavesdropping old man. Action, at last performed, had mocked him. His heart ached with horror and pity. "Thou wretched, rash, intruding fool," he mourned, "farewell. I took thee for thy better." He let fall the curtain and turned to his white-faced mother. "Peace, sit you down," he muttered, "and let me wring your heart."

She sank back upon the bed and tried, unavailingly, to shut her ears against such words as no son in all the world had ever stabbed a mother with. Tears made rivers in her cheeks and drowned her pearls as Hamlet pitilessly laid bare his mother's easy lust and the shameless corruption of her bed. Her husband-lover –

"A murderer and a villain!" accused Hamlet.

"No more," wept the Queen.

"A king of shreds and patches – "

Suddenly he fell silent. His looks altered and he seemed to stare into vacancy. He uttered words that made no sense.

"Alas, he's mad," breathed the Queen. She sat, not daring to move, till her son's fit should be over.

It was no madness that had suddenly stopped his tongue and engrossed his looks. The ghost had returned! The dead King's hopeless eyes dwelt forlornly on the bed, then fixed themselves upon the Prince.

"Do not forget," uttered the spirit. "This visitation is but to whet thy almost blunted purpose." Its bleak, unhappy gaze turned upon the trembling Queen.

"Speak to her, Hamlet," pleaded the dead King; as an aching memory of fondness stirred the ashes of his heart. Hamlet obeyed.

"How is it with you, lady?"

"Alas, how is't with you?" asked the Queen, who saw no ghost but only her mad son transfixed. "Whereon do you look?"

"On him, on him," cried Hamlet, pointing to his father and striving, with all his might, with all precise detail and exact picture, to make his mother see the figure by the bed. But all she saw were the bed's hangings, and Hamlet, mad.

"Why, look you there," cried the Prince, "look how it steals away. My father in his habit as he lived! Look where he goes even now out at the portal!" But she saw neither the ghost's coming, nor the ghost's going. It had not appeared to remind her of forgotten love, but to remind Hamlet of neglected revenge.

The scene had been strange and terrible and the King, had he heard of it, would have been filled with dread. But the quiet spy behind the curtain had overheard with an unrecording ear.

"This counsellor is now most still, most secret, and most grave," said Hamlet, as he dragged the dead Polonius from the room, "who was in life a foolish prating knave . . . Goodnight, mother."

He had hidden the body and would not confess where. It seemed he mocked his own bloody act by hiding the spy who could no more hide himself. Concealment had brought about Polonius's death; now death brought about his concealment. To all urgent questioning the Prince replied in a vein that was tragical-comical.

"Now, Hamlet, where's Polonius?"

"At supper."

"At supper? Where?"

"Not where he eats, but where a's eaten."

53

But soon the body was found and taken to the chapel. And, that very night, the mad and dangerous Prince was dispatched to England, in the close care of his good friends, Rosencrantz and Guildenstern. Dearly would the King have liked to dispatch him to join Polonius, but he dared not. The Queen's love for her son and the people's love for their Prince stood in his way. But England would serve his darker purpose. He entrusted, to Rosencrantz and Guildenstern, a sealed letter for the English King. In it he required that Hamlet should directly be put to death.

Ophelia begged to see the Queen. But the Queen was reluctant. Her soul was too burdened with her own griefs to endure the sight of Ophelia's. Nonetheless she was prevailed upon to see the girl, so Ophelia entered.

She wore, as was proper for her visit, her best and most delicate attire; but had buttoned it all awry, as if she knew she ought to be modest but could not recollect how. She had painted her cheeks, but one less skilfully than the other. Her hair was down and still wild from sleep for, although she had remembered to dress everything else, she had forgotten her head. Which was not to be wondered at: the murder of her father by her one-time lover had quite blown out the candle of her mind. She smiled absurdly at the Queen, and then began to sing. But there was more madness in her music than music in her madness, for she kept neither tune nor time. The songs she sang were lewd fragments and snatches that came weirdly from her lips. God knew what they meant to her, or where she'd gathered them, or for how long her modesty had kept them folded, like bride-gowns, at the bottom of her mind.

The King came in and, together with the Queen, looked on dismayed. "O Gertrude, Gertrude," he sighed to his wife, when the girl, with a dozen or more "Goodnights", had drifted meaninglessly away, "when sorrows come, they come not single spies, but in battalions . . ."

Laertes, the mad girl's brother and son of the murdered man, had returned from France and, even now, was in the city where rumour and discontent were inflaming his already unsteady nature. Bitterly the Queen began to reproach the unthinking insolence of the common people, when the sound of a furious commotion was heard. Doors splintered, steel clashed, and voices shouted. A moment after, Laertes, with sword drawn and some half-dozen wild-looking fellows at his heels, burst in. He glared about, saw the King, and bade his followers leave him and guard the door.

"O thou vile King!" he accused. "Give me my father!"

The Queen tried to hold him back.

"Let him go, Gertrude," said the King calmly. "Do not fear our person. There's such divinity doth hedge a king, that treason can but peep to what it would . . ."

Laertes faltered. Royalty awed him, and so did the thought of the King's Swiss guards. He took his advantage where it lay, and grew peaceable. Then Ophelia came back. As if reminded of a childish duty neglected, she had returned with a gift of flowers. She had gathered them from somewhere wild, for her gown was stained and torn and her white arms scratched. She smiled at her brother as if he was a stranger.

"O heavens," wept the young man, seeing the ruins of his sister, "is't possible a young maid's wits should be as mortal as an old man's life?"

She began to sing, no lewd fragments now, but the mournful ditty of a burying. Then she gave away her flowers, telling the proper virtue of each as she gave them to her brother, to the King, and to the Queen . . .

"There's rue for you. And here's some for me. We may call it herb of grace a Sundays. You must wear your rue with a difference," she said to the Queen, with an eerie cunning smile. She returned to singing, and presently, with a quick, "God be wi' you!" fled from the room.

The King, with cautious sympathy and enclosing arm, led the distressed brother aside, and promised to tell him how the tragedies had come about, and who had been to blame: not him – not him . . .

Two sailors, rough and slanting, with cutlasses wide enough to divide a man, brought a letter to Horatio, who had remained in Elsinore, and waited while he read it. The letter was from Hamlet. He was in Denmark. The vessel on which he'd sailed had been pursued by pirates. The ships had briefly grappled. Hamlet had boarded the pirate and been taken prisoner. His own ship had escaped and continued on to England. Since then he had come to terms with his captors. They were good fellows and would bring Horatio to where Hamlet now waited. Also, they had letters for the King.

At once, Horatio went with one of the sailors to meet with Hamlet, while the other took his letters to the King.

The King was still with Laertes. He had told the young man how Hamlet had murdered Polonius and had become dangerous to the throne itself. Laertes listened, and wondered why the King had done nothing against the murderer.

"Break not your sleeps for that," murmured the King, smiling his old smile that slipped round his lips like oil. "You shortly shall hear more . . ."

It was then that he was given the sailor's letter. Hastily he read it. Rage and amazement filled him. Hamlet was returned. Hamlet who should, by all the King's shrewd scheming, have been dead in England, was once more in Denmark. Tomorrow he would be coming to the court.

"Let him come!" begged Laertes, wild with hatred for his father's killer and longing only to destroy him. The King, desiring Hamlet's death no less, paced to and fro, brooding upon some means whereby this might be brought about, a means by which no blame should be laid at any door and even the Queen should think it an accident. His Queen was always in the front of his thoughts. His love for her was almost a sickness, equal with his guilt. He paused in his pacing, and beckoned Laertes to his side.

"What would you undertake," he asked softly, "to show yourself in deed your father's son more than in words?"

"To cut his throat i' the church!" came the prompt reply.

The King shook his head. The scheme he had in mind was different. Hamlet, who delighted in sword-play, was to be tempted into a fencing match with Laertes. One of the weapons would be unbated and needle-sharp. With this, Laertes might, as if by unlucky chance, kill his man. As he confided the scheme, the King watched the young man shrewdly, to see if so mean and dishonourable a proposal repelled him. But Laertes was Polonius's son, and guile and concealment were in his blood. He entered into the scheme with all his heart, and gilded its cunning with some of his own. He had brought back from France a deadly poison, and with this he'd anoint his sword. It was a poison for which there was no remedy, and the merest scratch would procure Hamlet's certain death. The King smiled. Poison was the means whereby he had gained his Queen and crown; it was fitting that poison should be the means whereby he secured them. It must be by poison. Therefore, if Laertes failed to wound the

57

Prince, a poisoned cup should be awaiting Hamlet when he paused to quench his thirst.

So Hamlet's death was encompassed; but even as it was nodded upon, there came news of another, lesser death. The weeping Queen came in to tell that Ophelia had been drowned. Frail mad Ophelia was dead. The news brought forth no wild excess of grief; but was received with quietness, as if this was calamity's fragile herald, sent in advance of its huge self.

A gravedigger was singing at his work. A jovial soul: the deeper he dug, the higher rose his spirits, and his song flew up in snatches, together with flying clods of earth. Hamlet and Horatio, on their way from the seashore to the castle, drew near; and the gravedigger, finding he had attracted a noble audience, paused, beamed, and wiped his brow. Amused by such good cheer among the bones, Hamlet fell into talk with the man; and Horatio could not but smile to see how his friend readily forgot his griefs and troubles in the pleasure of argument and debate, for the scholar-prince got as good as he gave. The gravedigger, by toiling so long among the grinners, had come by a shrewd and bony wit.

"What man dost thou dig it for?"

"For no man, sir."

"What woman, then?"

"For none neither."

"Who is to be buried in't?"

"One that was a woman, sir; but rest her soul, she's dead."

Presently he threw up a skull. Whose was it? Why, it was the old King's jester, Yorick . . .

"This?" murmured Hamlet, taking the skull in his hands and gazing at it, so that his sad smile was answered by its sightless grin.

"E'n that," said the gravedigger.

"Alas, poor Yorick," sighed the Prince. "I knew him, Horatio . . ." As Hamlet mused, the gravedigger continued with his work, for the grave's tenant was approaching to take possession of the premises. A sombre procession moved towards the grave, with a coffin borne on a swaying tide of black. The King and Queen were among the mourners: plainly the burial was for one of high estate. Hamlet and Horatio drew back, to observe the scene from a distance. The coffin was lowered into the earth, but the priest intoned no prayer; for the death had been doubtful. Suddenly, from among the mourners, Laertes stepped forward; and Hamlet saw that the grave he had laughed over had been made for Ophelia. He cried out in anguish; but his cry was quite lost in the shouted grief of Laertes, whose words and feelings were as extravagant as his attire. His black was a whole night to Hamlet's little corner of dark; his grieving was a tempest to Hamlet's aching sighs. Frantically he leaped down into the grave to catch up his sister for one last embrace; and Hamlet, enraged that Ophelia, whom he had loved, should be used as a property for such gaudy grief, rushed forward to grapple with Laertes in the grave. Fiercely they fought until they were dragged apart. Then Hamlet, much ashamed, retired with Horatio; and the burial of Ophelia was concluded.

"Strengthen your patience," murmured the King to Laertes, and reminded him that revenge would soon be his.

"So Guildenstern and Rosencrantz go to't," murmured Horatio. He and Hamlet were alone in the great hall of the castle; and Hamlet had told him how, on the ship bound for England, he had found, in the cabin of his two good schoolfriends, a sealed letter to be given to the English king. He had opened it and read therein his own death warrant. So he had, most skilfully, exchanged for another in which he had put forward Rosencrantz and Guildenstern in place of himself. Thus those two gentlemen had sailed on to England bearing with them, not Hamlet's, but their own deaths.

"Why, man, they did make love to this employment! They are not near my conscience," cried Hamlet, as if to defend himself against the sad regret he sensed in Horatio's words. Regret there certainly had been, not for Rosencrantz and Guildenstern, but for Hamlet himself. His was the tragedy, not theirs. Sadly Horatio gazed at the brilliant, lively and noble young Prince who had been dragged back into an ancient, corrupt world of poison, murder and revenge.

As they talked, there was a gust of perfume, a rustle of satins, and a courtier came into the hall. He was a delicate gentleman with a feathered bonnet and butterfly hands. He talked very roundabout, and with so many bows that his listeners marvelled at his flexibility. His message, when at last it was unravelled, was from the King, and was amiable enough. Having heard that, of late, Laertes had won a great reputation for fencing, and knowing Hamlet's fondness for the sport, the King had laid a wager on the outcome of a match between them – that is, if the Lord Hamlet was agreeable to trying his skill against Laertes. Thus appealed to, Hamlet could not refuse. He was proud of his skill as a swordsman and always eager for a chance to show it off.

"Sir, I will walk here in the hall," he informed the courtier. "Let the foils be brought, the gentleman willing, and the King hold his purpose, I will win for him and I can; if not, I will gain nothing but my shame and the odd hits."

When the courtier had departed, Hamlet frowned and shook his head. He knew not why, but a strange uneasiness had seized him.

"If your mind dislike anything, obey it," said Horatio anxiously. "I will forestall their repair hither and say you are not fit."

Hamlet smiled and shook his head. "We defy augury," he said. "There is special providence in the fall of a sparrow. If it be now, 'tis not to come; if it be not to come, it will be now; if it be not now, yet it will come. The readiness is all . . ."

Trumpets announced the approach of the King. The courtier had delivered his message promptly. The King and Queen entered the hall attended by all the court. Two servants carried a table, and a lord bore a bouquet of swords, like a bridesman of Death.

All was smiles and good humour, as if Hamlet's madness had never been. "Come, Hamlet, come," urged the affable King; and he drew the Prince and Laertes together so that they might clasp hands and seal their friendship in forgiveness.

"Give me your pardon, sir," said Hamlet warmly, for there was no enmity in his heart for Laertes. "I have done you wrong."

Laertes responded with equal generosity, and the King's smile broadened. The swords were offered. Laertes, being the quicker, chose first. "This is too heavy," he said with a frown, flourishing the weapon he had drawn. "Let me see another." Plainly he was a most fastidious swordsman. At length he found a blade to his satisfaction. The swords were offered to Hamlet, who cheerfully took the first that came. The two young men saluted each other in steel, and awaited the King's word for the bout to begin.

The King called for wine so that he might drink Hamlet's health should he win. The cups were filled and set upon the table. The King, with a royal gesture, held out a splendid pearl. If Laertes should be defeated, the pearl would be cast into Hamlet's cup of wine. The court murmured, and applauded the magnificence of the prize.

"Come, begin!" exclaimed the King. "And you, the judges, bear a wary eye."

Swords touched, and the judges, two dancing, skipping, hopping courtiers, followed the weaving blades. The fencers, both in black, for each mourned a murdered father, circled one another, made swift lunges, darted back, lunged again, parried, thrust, riposted –

"One!" cried Hamlet, triumphantly.

"No!" cried Laertes.

The judges were appealed to, and declared: "A hit, a very palpable hit."

"Well, again!" demanded Laertes.

"Stay," ordered the King. "Give me drink. Hamlet, this pearl is thine." He cast it into Hamlet's cup, and offered it to the Prince. But Hamlet would not drink. He would try another bout first. He and Laertes fenced again; and again Hamlet scored a hit.

"Our son shall win," said the King. The Queen smiled proudly, and offered her son her napkin to wipe his sweating brow.

"The Queen carouses to thy fortune, Hamlet," she said, and took a cup of wine.

"Gertrude, do not drink!" muttered the King, his face grey with horror.

"I will, my lord," said she. "I pray you pardon me."

The cup she held was Hamlet's cup. She drank the poison that had been laid for her son.

"My lord, I'll hit him now!" whispered Laertes to the King.

"I do not think it," said the King, whose eyes were upon his poisoned Queen, and whose whole world was beginning to crack and crumble about him.

"Have at you now!" shouted Laertes, seeing Hamlet unprepared. He thrust at him, and caught him on the wrist. Hamlet looked down amazed. He was bleeding.

Laertes' sword had been unbated! He looked up at Laertes and saw guilt and hatred in his eyes. Bewilderment, then fury seized him. Though he never knew it, he had been fighting for his life. Savagely he flung himself upon Laertes, and beat the weapon from his hand. He picked it up, and contemptuously flung Laertes his own. They fought again: Laertes in terror, and Hamlet with all the skill at his command.

"Part them," cried out the King, "they are incensed!"

"Nay, come again!" shouted Hamlet, and, with a sudden thrust, pierced Laertes through.

Now the poison was spread, the poison that had, so long, rotted away the castle of Elsinore; and it was a poison, like the venom Laertes had brought back, for which there was no remedy. The Queen, the easy, lustful Queen, felt agony seize her. She cried out: "The drink, the drink! O my dear Hamlet! The drink, the drink! I am poisoned!" She fell back, and with lifeless eyes stared at her son.

"Let the door be locked!" shouted Hamlet. "Treachery! Seek it out!"

"It is here, Hamlet," sighed Laertes, bleeding from his wound, and dying from the venom of his own blade. "Hamlet, thou art slain. No medicine in the world can do thee good; in thee there is not half an hour's life . . ." So Laertes, while there was still breath in him, confessed his treachery, and pointed to the one whose crime, like Cain's, had brought about so many deaths. "The King – the King's to blame."

There was no delaying now, no breathing time for thought. With a terrible cry, Hamlet rushed upon the King and stabbed him with his sword. But, like a serpent, the King would not die.

"Here, thou incestuous, murderous, damned Dane, drink off this potion!" the avenger cried and forced the poisoned cup between the King's unresisting lips, and made him drink. "Follow my mother!"

"He is justly served," breathed Laertes; and with the last of his life, begged forgiveness of Hamlet for what he had done. Like Hamlet, he had avenged his father; and, like Hamlet, he died for it.

"I follow thee," murmured Hamlet, over the young man who now lay quiet and still. "I am dead, Horatio," he whispered to his friend who had come forward to support him. He trembled as a chill began to invade him. Then he smiled ruefully. "This fell sergeant, Death, is strict in his arrest . . ."

There came a sound of martial music and gunfire from outside the castle walls. A messenger entered, to tell that Fortinbras, the victorious Prince of Norway, was approaching. With a last effort, Hamlet roused himself. He was a Prince, and his concerns were now with the state, good order, and the well-being of his people. "The election lights on Fortinbras. He has my dying voice," decreed the Prince. Then, all strength spent, he fell back in Horatio's arms. "The rest is silence," he sighed.

Through veils and veils of tears, Horatio gazed down upon the quiet countenance that rested against his arm. "Good night, sweet Prince, and flights of angels sing thee to thy rest."

It was thus that Fortinbras found them, the dead and those who still lived, in the great hall of the castle of Elsinore.

"Let four captains bear Hamlet like a soldier to the stage," said Fortinbras, when he had heard Hamlet's story, "for he was likely, had he been put on, to have proved most royal . . ." The captains lifted up the dead Prince and carried him away. "Go, bid the soldiers shoot," commanded Fortinbras; and solemn gunfire roared in honour of the Prince of Denmark.

As You Like It

It began upon a winter's morning in an orchard in France. A cold sun was slanting down between the naked trees, and a cold wind was making them shiver and shake their skinny fists at an unnatural Nature that had stripped them of their clothing when most they had need of it. At the same time a poorly dressed young man was pacing back and forth, and likewise shaking his fists at an unnatural Nature. Against all the obligations of blood, his eldest brother had cheated him out of his rights and left him to stink in the mire like a beast of the field!

"His horses are bred better!" he cried out bitterly. "I will no longer endure it!"

A withered old tree – or so, at first glance, it seemed – creaked into motion and laid a comforting branch upon the young man's sleeve. It was an aged servant by the name of Adam, who, by his bent back and his pecked and wrinkled cheeks, might have been that very Adam who had been booted out of Eden. Sadly, he shook his frosty head. The lad was right, and it was a bad business. If ever a lad had just cause for complaint, it was Orlando, the youngest son of good Sir Rowland de Boys. Even before the old gentleman had been cold in his grave, Oliver, the eldest son and the new master, had shoved Orlando from his rightful place at table, and lorded it over the estate alone. Truly, the world had fallen away from the goodly place it once had been . . .

Suddenly, a shadow fell across the path. "Yonder comes my master, your brother!" warned the old man as Oliver, swaggering in furs and velvet, appeared among the trees. As quickly as he could, the old servant took himself off and watched, from a little distance, the meeting of the brothers: the one, a rich and costly gentleman, the other, a rough-hewn peasant in coarse woollen, with anger in his eyes like a half-smothered fire in straw, threatening a sudden blaze. Nor was it long in coming! Angry words passed between them, then Oliver shouted: "What, boy!" and raised his hand to strike his brother!

"Sweet masters, be patient!" cried out Adam, rushing forward to prevent murder being done, for Orlando had seized his brother's wrist, twisted his arm behind his back, and secured him with an elbow around his throat! And all in an instant! Already Oliver's face was purple with choking, as he kicked and struggled like a dog in a sack. "For your father's remembrance, be at accord!" pleaded Adam; but Orlando would not let his brother go until he had squeezed a promise out of him that his inheritance would be paid.

"And what wilt thou do? Beg, when that is spent?" muttered Oliver savagely, rubbing his bruised throat and his bruised arm. "Leave me!" His eye fell upon the old servant. "Get you with him, you old dog!"

"Is 'old dog' my reward?" protested Adam indignantly. "Most true, I have lost my teeth in your service. God be with my old master! He would not have spoke such a word!" Then, seeing Orlando's fists clench in anger at such treatment of a faithful servant, and fearing more violence, he tugged him away.

There was someone waiting to speak with Sir Oliver de Boys. A strange visitor indeed. A mountainous fellow, who might have broken the back of a bear with his powerful arms, or killed a lion with one blow of his

66

huge fist. He was Monsieur Charles, the Duke's wrestler, and the strongest man in France. Despite his great strength, the wrestler was a humble fellow and easily tongue-tied in the presence of a gentleman of rank.

"Good Monsieur Charles," said Oliver pleasantly, and meaning to put the fellow at his ease, "what's the new news at the new court?"

"There's no news at the court, sir, but the old news," answered the wrestler; and then, gaining courage, went on to tell that the new Duke was still the new Duke, and his elder brother, whom he had overthrown, had fled for safety into the Forest of Arden, "and a many merry men with him," he related with growing eloquence; "and there they live like the old Robin Hood of England. They say many young gentlemen flock to him every day, and fleet the time carelessly as they did in the golden world." He paused, and a small sigh crept out of him, like a mouse coming forth from a mountain . . .

"You wrestle tomorrow before the new Duke?" inquired Oliver, impatient to bring the fellow out of the golden world and to the purpose of his visit, which, he supposed, must be to do with his trade. He was not mistaken. At once, a deeply serious look came over Monsieur Charles's large countenance, and Oliver, his heart beating rapidly, listened in silence as the wrestler unburdened his troubled spirit. He had heard that, among the foolhardy youth who had put themselves forward to challenge him, there was none other than his lordship's own younger brother, Orlando! It was for this reason that he had come. Earnestly, he begged his lordship to persuade his brother against so foolish a course. He, Charles, had no wish to break the young gentleman's limbs.

"I had as lief," murmured Oliver, "thou didst break his neck as his finger!" And, as Monsieur Charles

67

looked amazed at so unbrotherly a wish, he went on to represent Orlando as so black and treacherous a villain, that it would be a good deed to rid the world of him!

Monsieur Charles sighed with relief. "I'll give him his payment," he promised; and, as the huge fellow departed, well-pleased to be doing his lordship a service, Oliver smiled with satisfaction. He hated his brother with all his heart; and for no stronger reason than that Orlando had always been loved better than himself. But it was reason enough . . .

The new court, like a woman in a new gown, was proud, but inclined to be uneasy, as if wondering if all was secure behind. This shadow of unease had even darkened the ordinarily high spirits of the two young women who walked together in the great hall of the new Duke's palace. They were Princesses, both. One was Celia, daughter of Frederick, the new Duke; the other was Rosalind, daughter of his brother, the overthrown Duke in the forest. Although Duke Frederick had protested that he loved Rosalind as tenderly as he loved his own daughter, it was impossible for Rosalind to forget her dearly loved father, living like an outlaw in Arden.

"I pray thee, Rosalind," pleaded Celia, for the hundredth time, "be merry!" But neither she nor Touchstone, the court jester – a fellow who, in his own opinion, could have squeezed laughter out of a lemon – could persuade her into more than the mouse of a smile, and a promise that she would try to do better.

"Here comes Monsieur Le Beau!" said Celia; and Rosalind's smile did indeed grow a little as that willowy gentleman of the court wafted towards them, like a flower in velvet boots.

"Fair Princess," he cried, addressing Celia with a

twinkle of yellow stockings and a sweep of his feathered hat, "you have lost much good sport!"

"Sport?" inquired Celia, upon which the courtier eagerly informed the ladies that Monsieur Charles, the Duke's wrestler, had already broken the ribs of three young men who had been rash enough to answer his challenge. And the ladies had missed it!

"It is the first time," marvelled Touchstone, "that ever I heard breaking of ribs was sport for ladies!" But Monsieur Le Beau, ignoring the jester, assured the Princesses that they had not missed all. The best was yet to come. Another young man had come forward –

Even as he spoke, there was a murmuring commotion and the Duke and his court flowed into the great hall like a perfumed silken tide. Among them towered the huge figure of Monsieur Charles and, beside him, like a frail sapling next to a mighty oak, walked the new challenger, a humbly dressed youth whose proud looks and straight limbs made the heart ache for the ruin that was to become of them. It was Orlando.

Celia heard a sigh, a sigh that was deep enough to drown a world in. She turned. Her cousin was gazing, with enormous eyes, at the doomed young man; and her face was pale as death. "Alas," she whispered, "he is too young!"

Nor was Rosalind the only one to be affected. Duke Frederick himself had sought to persuade the young man from his foolhardy course; but to no avail. "Speak to him, ladies," he urged his daughter and his niece; "see if you can move him."

So Orlando was brought before the two Princesses who, one after another, begged him to abandon the unequal contest.

"Do, young sir!" pleaded Rosalind, and with a passion that seemed, to Celia, to have been stirred by something stronger than a mere wish to please the Duke. But the young man was resolved. He declared it

did not matter to him whether he lived or died ...
although his eyes, as he gazed at Rosalind, seemed, to
the curious Celia, to tell a very different tale. "The
little strength that I have, I would it were with you!"
breathed Rosalind, as the young man bowed to the two
Princesses and departed to do battle with the cruel giant.

Rosalind could not bear to watch. She covered her
face with her hands. But, at the same time, could not
bear *not* to watch, and her eyes kept sparkling through
a lattice-work of fingers. "You shall try but one fall,"
she heard the Duke command; and she glimpsed the
wide seated circle of the eager court.

"But come your ways!" the young man shouted
defiantly; and the contest began!

She shut her eyes. She could hear grunts and gasps
and cries, and the scrape and thump of staggering feet
... She opened her eyes ... caught a sudden sight of
the giant's face, swollen with fierce triumph ... then
the young man, his poor head in a halter of mighty
arms. The Duke was leaning forward, his fists were
tightly clenched. A lady of the court had fainted clean
away; a gentleman was sprinkling her with water, and
a lady by her side was frantically tugging to free her
gown. There was a loud cry! Then came a great shout.
The Duke was on his feet, amazed –

Fearfully, Rosalind took her hands away from her
face. She stared. "O excellent young man!" she cried
out. Most marvellously, he was standing upright and
unharmed! Beside him, like a fallen mountain, lay
Monsieur Charles. The contest was ended. The youth
had overthrown the giant!

Everyone was on their feet and applauding, and,
while half a dozen servants carried the groaning
Charles away, the Duke himself, all smiles, was shaking the young man by the hand and asking his name.
"Orlando, my liege," he answered proudly; "the youngest son of Sir Rowland de Boys."

At once, the Duke let go of his hand. Sir Rowland de Boys had been the good friend of the Duke in the forest; therefore his son was the new Duke's enemy. In an instant, smiles were changed to frowns, and joy to darkness and anger. "I would thou hadst told me of another father," he said abruptly, and departed from the hall, with the suddenly alarmed court hastening after.

Orlando and the two Princesses were alone in the great hall, with some awkward yards of silence between them.

"Let us go thank him," said Celia, feeling that, if she did not speak, her cousin and the young man would remain motionless, like two posts in a field, for ever and a day. Gently but firmly she urged Rosalind forward.

"Gentleman," murmured Rosalind, "wear this for me." And, impulsively taking a gold chain from her neck, offered it to Orlando. He stared at it. Impatiently, Rosalind put it over his head; and then, overcome with confusion at her own boldness, she turned to Celia. "Shall we go, coz?"

"Ay. Fare you well, fair gentleman," said Celia with a smile, and took her cousin by the arm.

They were half-way to vanishing from the hall before Orlando recovered the power of speech.

"Can I not say, I thank you?" he whispered, marvelling at the suddenness of the affliction that had struck him dumb.

"He calls us back!" cried Rosalind, catching the whisper and dragging Celia nearly off her feet in her haste to return. "Did you call, sir?" she asked eagerly; but Orlando was speechless again. "Sir, you have wrestled well, and overthrown more than your enemies," she went on, with such warmth in her voice and honesty in her eyes that a stone would have been moved to speak. But not Orlando.

"Will you go, coz?" murmured Celia, seeing it was a hopeless case. Reluctantly, Rosalind agreed, and with a sad shake of her head, accompanied her cousin out of the hall. Helplessly, the young man gazed after her.

"O poor Orlando," he sighed, "thou art overthrown!" The God of Love had shot him, not with a single arrow, but with his whole quiverful!

But the God of Hate was also aiming his arrows at Orlando. He felt a touch upon his shoulder. Startled, he turned. Monsieur Le Beau, on his velvet feet, had tiptoed up beside him. "Good sir," muttered the courtier, with anxious looks behind, "I do in friendship counsel you to leave this place!" Orlando frowned in puzzlement, and the courtier went on to confide that the Duke, who trusted no one, had suddenly taken it into his head that the youngest son of Sir Rowland de Boys was a threat to him. "Sir, fare you well," he urged; and, as he spoke, the mask of smiles that he, like everyone else in the new Duke's court habitually wore, slipped to reveal an honest man with an honest care for the young man's safety. "Hereafter, in a better world than this," he murmured softly, "I shall desire more love and knowledge of you."

Orlando thanked him warmly; and, cursing the cruelty of fortune that had offered him love with one hand only to snatch it back with the other, he hastened away. Sadly, Monsieur Le Beau watched him go; then, adjusting his courtier's mask of smiles, he trotted off to wait upon his master.

The Duke was in a fever of enemies. He saw them all around him. Every smile hid a frown; every word of love hid a thought of hate. No one was beyond suspicion; and least of all Rosalind, the daughter of the brother he had wronged, and whose presence in the court he had only tolerated on account of the love his own daughter had for her. But that was all over –

"Mistress!" he shouted, bursting into the apartment where his daughter and the hated one were laughing together. "Get you from our court!"

"Me, uncle?" cried Rosalind, amazed.

"You!" answered the Duke in a mounting rage; and he swore that if she should be found within twenty miles of the court, she would die for it! Celia, outraged by her father's cruel injustice, declared that she would go wherever her cousin went.

"You are a fool!" said the Duke contemptuously; and, with his palely smiling courtiers, swept out of the room.

The cousins stared at one another in fear and stark amazement. "Whither shall we go?" whispered Rosalind at length.

"To seek my uncle in the Forest of Arden," decided Celia, without hesitation.

The forest! At once, the image of a dark and dreadful place of savage beasts and lurking robbers presented itself to the cousins' imagination. Surely it was no place for a pair of tender Princesses! "I'll put myself in poor and mean attire," proposed Celia. "The like do you."

"Were it not better," suggested Rosalind, "because I am more than common tall, that I do suit me all points like a man?" So it was agreed: Rosalind, in man's attire, would be known as Ganymede, and Celia, dressed like a shepherdess, would be his sister, Aliena. Then Rosalind had another thought. Should they not take Touchstone, the court jester, with them for company?

Celia nodded. "He'll go along o'er the wide world with me," she promised; and straightway the cousins set about making ready for their flight.

While the two Princesses, in secret haste, were stuffing their purses with gold and their satchels with clothing, and Touchstone, gnawing his fingernails, was waiting below their window to steady the ladder for their night-time descent, Orlando, that other victim of the Duke's frantic suspicions, returned to his lodging.

As he approached, all was dark. A shadow stirred. "Who's there?"

It was old Adam, his face as white as his hair. "O unhappy youth, come not within these doors!" he cried out, barring Orlando's path. In a shaking voice, he warned the young man that his brother Oliver, enraged by his success, meant to burn down his lodging that very night, with the sleeping Orlando inside it! "This house is but a butchery," he whispered. "Do not enter it!"

Orlando, his life now threatened in his own home, asked bitterly what was to become of him: must he get his living by robbing on the highway, or by begging in the town? The old servant shook his head. He had five hundred crowns, he said, that he had saved up during his long years of service; and now at last he had found a better use for his little fortune than ever he could have supposed. He offered it to Orlando and asked no more in return than that the young man should take him as his servant. "Though I look old, yet I am strong and lusty," he protested, as Orlando looked sadly at his white hair and frail limbs. "Let me go with you; I'll do the service of a younger man . . ."

"O good old man!" cried Orlando, his eyes filling up with tears. "Thou art not for the fashion of these times, where none will sweat but for promotion . . ." Adam bowed his head. "But come thy ways," said Orlando with a smile, "we'll go along together!" and with lifting hearts and sturdy pace, they set off side by side into the night.

The palace was in an uproar! The Princesses had gone, and the jester with them! Their beds had been unslept in, and none knew when or where they had fled. All that could be found out was from a gentlewoman who had overheard the Princesses warmly praising the youth who had overthrown the wrestler. Find that youth, was her shrewd advice, and you will find the others.

"Fetch that gallant hither!" commanded the Duke. "If he be absent, bring his brother!" and, as frightened courtiers hastened to obey, the search went on, high and low, for the runaways.

The day was ending, and in the forest the gathering gloom turned every tree into a lurking robber, and every bush into a bear. "O Jupiter, how merry are my spirits!" cried Rosalind, for all the world as if she meant it; but her companions were not of her mind.

"I care not for my spirits, if my legs were not weary," groaned Touchstone, his melancholy countenance drooping onto the bright patchwork of his jester's coat; and Celia, a Princess of burrs and scratches, limping far behind, wailed:

"I pray you, bear with me: I can go no further."

"Well, this is the Forest of Arden!" said Rosalind, determined to be cheerful; for now she was in man's attire, with her golden hair crammed up inside her feathered cap, she was resolved, against all private inclination, to be a prop and a comfort to her frailer friends.

"Ay, now am I in Arden," moaned Touchstone, sitting down on a tree-stump and nursing his blistered feet, "the more fool I; when I was at home I was in a better place – "

There came a sound of footfalls and a murmur of voices! The three travellers looked to one another in alarm; and then, forgetful of their aching limbs, skipped, brisk as lambs, into the concealment of the trees.

No sooner had they vanished from the clearing, than two inhabitants of the forest appeared. They proved to be nothing more alarming than a pair of shepherds: one sturdy and grey-haired; the other, young and tender, and full of sighs. They were talking of love, and the elder was gently advising his young companion against being too slavish in his courtship of his beloved. But his words went unheeded. "O Corin," cried the afflicted one, clapping a hand to his pale brow, "that thou knew'st how I do love her!"

"I partly guess," smiled Corin, "for I have loved ere now." But the youth would not have it. He could not believe that any man had loved as he loved, and not bear the scars for all to see.

"Thou hast not loved!" he cried indignantly; and, clutching his hair as if to pull it out by the roots, rushed off into the forest, calling: "O Phebe, Phebe, Phebe!" to the unfeeling bushes and trees.

Rosalind, in concealment, felt an ache in her heart. The shepherd's passion for his Phebe reminded her sharply of her own for Orlando; and such was the power of visible love, that even the ever-mocking Touchstone was driven to recollect a time when he, too, had been laid low by the same madness. "We that are true lovers," he sighed, "run into strange capers."

Celia alone felt differently. True, she felt pangs; but they were in her stomach, not in her heart. "I pray you," she begged, "one of you question yond man, if he for gold will give us any food: I faint almost to death."

"Holla, you clown!" called out Touchstone, with a courtier's contempt for simple countrymen who were little better than the beasts they tended.

"Who calls?" asked Corin; and he stared in wonderment as the trees disgorged themselves of strange fruit indeed: a haughty jester, a lady dressed as a shepherdess who, he would have taken his oath, had never tended sheep save with a knife and spoon, as mutton, and a swaggering young huntsman with villainous sword and fearsome spear, whose complexion was as soft as a flower.

"Good even to you, friend," said the huntsman, with a mildness that belied his fierce ironmongery; and he went on to beg, for his fainting sister's sake, food and shelter for which he was willing to pay. Sadly, Corin shook his head. He was not his own master, but served a man who cared nothing for hospitality, and wanted only to sell his cottage, pasture and flock, and have done with them.

On hearing this, the young huntsman glanced at his sister; and she, poor famished soul, eagerly nodded her head. Without more ado, the huntsman offered to buy the property and pay Corin his wages for tending the sheep. "Assuredly the thing is to be sold," said Corin, well pleased at the prospect of so pleasant and monied a young master; and they all went off together, new landlords of a piece of Arden.

But in another part of the forest, two travellers were not so fortunate. They had journeyed far, and one, the elder, was almost at his end. "Dear master, I can go no further," gasped old Adam, his piled-up years at last overcoming his willing spirit. "O I die for food. Here lie I down," he sighed, sinking to the ground, "and measure out my grave. Farewell, kind master."

"Why, how now, Adam?" cried Orlando, rushing back to help the old man, "no greater heart in thee?" Desperately he chafed the old man's freezing hands and smoothed his brow. He gathered moss and leaves to make a pillow for his head, and laid his coat over the old man to keep him warm. "Live a little; comfort a little!" he pleaded; and hoping that the habit of long service would make the old servant obey, he sternly bade him keep death away while he, Orlando, went in search of food. "Thou shalt not die for lack of a dinner," he promised, and, drawing his sword, set off into the forest. "Cheerly, good Adam!" he called back encouragingly, but could not subdue the dread in his heart that when he returned, old Adam would no longer be alive.

As he crept among the darkening trees, he paused from time to time to listen for a rustling, or the crackling of a twig, that would betray some wild creature that would serve them for food. But the forest was as quiet as a grave. Then, suddenly, he heard, very faintly, a strange sound. He strained his ears. It was a voice, singing! With beating heart, he hastened towards it . . .

> "Under the greenwood tree
> Who loves to lie with me . . ."

It was a young man's voice, full of easy confidence, and seemed to be moving from place to place. Eagerly Orlando followed it, sometimes mistaking the echo for the substance, but ever drawing nearer . . .

"Come hither, come hither, come hither," tempted the wandering voice,

> "Here shall he see
> No enemy
> But winter and rough weather
> Come hither, come hither . . ."

Stumbling over roots, scratched and torn by spiteful branches, Orlando pursued the song. Suddenly, it ceased. Lanterns were gleaming among the trees, and there was a murmur of voices. Orlando stopped, amazed.

In a golden clearing, like a little summer's day, a company of outlaws were gathered together; and in their midst were spread enough good things to eat to save a dozen dying men! With a wildly desperate cry, Orlando rushed into the clearing, fiercely brandishing his sword. "Forbear, and eat no more!"

The outlaws turned in astonishment. "Why, I have eat none yet," protested one, a long-faced melancholy fellow, pointing to his empty plate. Then another, who, from the respect accorded him, seemed to be the leader of the band, reproached Orlando for his show of needless force. "What would you have?" he asked courteously.

"I almost die for food," answered Orlando; to which the other replied: "Sit down and feed, and welcome to our table."

Strange forest! where fury was answered by gentleness, and outlaws spoke with the tongues of kindness! Ashamed, Orlando laid his sword aside. "There is an old poor man," he told them, "who after me hath many a weary step limped in pure love. Till he be first sufficed I will not touch a bit."

"Go find him out," said the leader kindly, "and we will nothing waste till you return."

"I thank ye!" cried Orlando, weeping with gratitude, and hastened back to his old servant, praying with all his heart that he would not be too late.

"Thou seest we are not all alone unhappy," observed the Duke when the wild young man had gone; for this leader of the outlaw band was indeed the banished Duke, and the outlaws gathered round him were the young men who had flocked to join him and live the greenwood life. "This wide and universal theatre," continued the philosophical Duke, "presents more woeful pageants than the scene wherein we play in."

"All the world's a stage," instantly observed the melancholy one, whose name was Jacques, "and all the men and women merely players. They have their exits and their entrances, and one man in his time plays many parts, his acts being seven ages." He paused and, picking up his empty plate, polished it on his sleeve till it shone like a mirror, and studied his reflection. Then, suiting his expression to his words, he expounded the seven ages of man, from, "the infant, mewling and puking in the nurse's arms" and continuing on his relentless journey to the grave, concluding with, "second childishness and mere oblivion, sans teeth, sans eyes, sans taste, sans everything."

But no sooner had his bleak and dreadful vision of man's old age been presented, than, in an instant it was overthrown! Orlando returned, bearing old Adam on his back. The good old man had obeyed his young master, and remained alive! Here was the visible evidence of age not useless, but wonderfully enriched by courage, loyalty and love! "Welcome!" cried the Duke, mightily glad to see it. "Set down your venerable burden and let him feed!"

At once, willing hands assisted the old man to a place at the feast, and helped him to food; and, while his guests were satisfying their hunger, the Duke called for music, and the singer who had been heard in the forest, obliged the company with another song.

> "Blow, blow, thou winter wind,
> Thou art not so unkind
> As man's ingratitude,"

he sang, while the courtiers in the forest sighed and nodded: it was a truth they had learned only too well.

> "Then heigh-ho! the holly!
> This life is most jolly!"

and all were agreed.

Even as Orlando found gentleness in the savage forest, so his brother Oliver found savagery in the gentle court. The maddened Duke Frederick, still seeking his daughter, had learned that Orlando had also fled. "Find out thy brother!" he shouted at the fearful Oliver. "Bring him dead or living within this twelvemonth!" and, with bloodshot eye and direst threats, despatched him to obey or lose all that he possessed. So Oliver, like many another bewildered by sudden adversity, turned his desperate steps towards the Forest of Arden . . .

A strange malady had begun to afflict the trees of the forest. It first appeared as Touchstone and the good countryman Corin were walking together, near to the cottage that Celia and Rosalind had newly bought. "Here comes young Master Ganymede," said Corin, interrupting the jester's unending flow of wit as Rosalind, still in her man's attire, came winding slowly among the trees. She was deep in the study of a paper, and, unaware of her audience, was reading aloud:

"From the East to western Ind,
No jewel is like Rosalind . . ."

"This is the very false gallop of verses!" cried Touchstone, unable to endure such poor stuff. "Why do you infect yourself with them?"

"Peace, you dull fool!" cried Rosalind, blushing to have been overheard reciting her own praises. "I found them on a tree."

"Truly, the tree yields bad fruit!" said the jester, to which Rosalind returned as good as she got, and the battle of wits would have continued had not another deep reader appeared among the trees. It was Celia, likewise with her nose in a paper that declared still more wonders of Rosalind.

"O most gentle Jupiter!" protested Rosalind (when it

was plain there was no more to come), "what tedious homily of love . . ."

Startled, Celia turned, to discover an audience crowding at her heels. She was no better pleased than Rosalind at being overheard reciting, not her own praises, but another's. Sharply, she dismissed the jester and the countryman. Then she turned to Rosalind and held out the paper. "Didst thou hear these verses?" Humbly Rosalind confessed she had, but hastened to add that she did not think highly of them. Celia gazed at her cousin thoughtfully; and asked if she had not wondered how it had come about that half the trees in the forest had been stricken by the same poetic malady? Again, Rosalind confessed it, and held out her own paper in evidence. Celia ignored it, and inquired if Rosalind knew who had hung up her name so far and wide?

"Is it a man?" ventured Rosalind, striving to keep a mounting excitement out of her voice.

Celia nodded. "And a chain," she said, striving to keep a bubbling up of laughter out of hers, "that you once wore, about his neck. Change you colour?"

A needless question. At once Rosalind began to plague Celia for more particulars, which Celia laughingly withheld, like sweets from a child, until, having been pursued round trees and bushes by her wildly importuning cousin, she gave up and confessed that the poet had been none other than the young man who had wrestled so well: Orlando! But far from contenting her, the news drove Rosalind at first into a frantic dismay that Orlando should see her in man's attire and not at her best, and then into another tempest of questioning that was only stopped when Celia cried: "Soft! comes he not here?"

Rosalind's eyes grew huge. "'Tis he!" she whispered, and jerked Celia into concealment as her beloved approached.

He was not alone. He was walking with a long-faced melancholy fellow, a wretch who was daring to complain that Orlando's love-songs were spoiling the trees. But Orlando defended his verses with spirit. "Rosalind is your love's name?" the wretch inquired; and, on receiving confirmation, most impertinently declared, "I do not like her name!"

To which Orlando justly replied, "There was no thought of pleasing you when she was christened!" The fellow sniffed and asked, "What stature is she of?"

"Just as high as my heart!" came back the answer, which, in Rosalind's opinion, could not have been bettered by any man. At length, they parted with expressions of mutual disdain, and Orlando was left alone.

"I will speak to him like a saucy lackey!" determined Rosalind; and, before Celia could stop her, she had strutted out with a swagger and a manly frown. Uneasily, Celia followed. She could not believe the young man would fail to recognize his Rosalind, no matter what she wore. But love proved blind, not only to the loved one's faults, but to her virtues as well! True, once or twice he looked curiously at 'Master Ganymede', as if a recollection was stirring; but it was plain he never saw, in the impudently posturing youth before him, the gently bred Princess of the court.

"I pray you, what is't o'clock?" she began; and thereafter Celia was lost in wonderment as she found herself audience to the strangest courtship in the world! Lacking the assistance of a gorgeous gown, rich golden hair and speaking eyes, Rosalind had only her wit with which to dazzle her lover, to entangle and bewitch him with a thousand whirling words. "Love is merely a madness," she was saying, having at last, like a skilful shepherd, guided her unruly flock of words to that very subject; "yet I profess curing it by counsel."

"I would not be cured, youth," sighed Orlando; upon which, Rosalind, concealing her joy, insisted that her remedy at least be tried. Then, sailing so near to the wind of discovery that Celia held her breath, she proposed that Orlando call her Rosalind and come to court her every day, when she would be so wild, so fantastical, so changeable and contrary in her moods, that the very name of Rosalind would become a torment rather than a delight. "And this way I will take it upon me," she promised, "to wash your liver as clean as a sound sheep's heart that there shall not be one spot of love in't!" Orlando smiled at the youth's confidence, but assured him that the remedy would have no success. But Rosalind insisted, and Orlando, with a laugh, gave in. "With all my heart, good youth!"

"Nay," cried Rosalind, raising her hand in stern rebuke, "you must call me Rosalind!" and, extending a brotherly arm to Celia, stalked away before solemnity was blown to the winds.

Love lay upon the forest like a blight. The very trees, as if they had sucked in sugar from the verses that had been hung upon them, seemed to twine together in gnarly embraces; and Jacques, who had just parted from one love-sick fool, now found himself witness to a pair of them, like cock and hen, crowing in a glade. One was a fool by nature, the other, a fool by profession.

Touchstone, wearied of country life, and finding nothing to aim his wit at, save a few sagely nodding bushes and a philosophical sheep or two, had decided to take unto himself a wife. It seemed to be in the fashion, and he was nothing if not fashionable. He had chosen, for this high office, one Audrey, a country wench, thick of speech and stinking like a goat. The union suited him very well. As male and female, they agreed as readily as the beasts of the field; and as courtier and foul slut, they were worlds apart. In this manner, he found satisfaction both as a man and as a gentleman: for Audrey never understood a word he said and, accordingly, held him in high respect. But yet there were moments when he could not help having his doubts . . .

"Truly," he sighed, gazing at Audrey, whose mouth stood open, like a kitchen door, blasting forth stale cabbage and onions, "I would the gods had made thee poetical."

"I do not know what 'poetical' is," pleaded Audrey, humbled by the wondrous mystery of language. "Is it honest in deed and word? Is it a true thing?"

"No, truly, for the truest poetry is the most feigning," returned Touchstone; then, perceiving that his pearls had been cast away, sadly shook his head. "But be it as it may be," he sighed, having weighed Audrey against a lonely life, which was something against nothing, "I will marry thee." And Audrey laughed and clapped her hands. "Well, the gods give us joy!" she cried.

Orlando had not come. The morning sun, bursting through the forest in misty beams and sudden glares, made a thousand flickering phantoms of him; but none proved real, and Rosalind, disgracing her man's attire, wept. Celia, who knew nothing of the pangs of true love, tried to comfort her cousin by abusing Orlando for lack of constancy –

"Nay, certainly, there is no truth in him," she declared.

"Not true in love?" wailed Rosalind.

"Yes, when he is in," said Celia; "but I think he is not in."

"But you heard him swear downright he was!"

"'Was' is not 'is'," pointed out Celia, and would have

said a great deal more, had not their shepherd, old Corin, interrupted the argument.

He came in haste, his weathered face all aglow. With twinkling merriment, he told his mistress and his master of an entertainment nearby in the forest that was well worth their attendance. The young shepherd, who, as they remembered, was so in love that he was almost dying of it, was even now pleading his cause before his Phebe! "Go hence a little," he urged, "and I shall conduct you . . ."

"O! come," cried Rosalind eagerly: "the sight of lovers feedeth those in love!" and the cousins followed after the beckoning old countryman.

The lovers were in a clearing, like a tragical picture framed in tangled hawthorn and sharp briar. The young shepherd, whose name was Silvius, was on his knees before his Phebe, who sat on a tree-stump, a rustic queen upon a rustic throne. "Sweet Phebe, do not scorn me!" he pleaded; while she, proud impossible she, her black eyes sparking like coals in a grate, dealt him blow after blow of sovereign disdain.

At length, Rosalind could endure her unkindness and arrogance no longer. "Who might be your mother," she cried, striding into the clearing and confronting the lofty shepherdess, "that you insult, exult, and all at once, over the wretched?"

The wretched fell over backwards, and the rustic queen gaped in amazement at the sudden youth whose eyes out-flashed her own. Quite dazzled, she sat in silence as he indignantly rebuked her for her pride. Nor was Silvius spared. "You foolish shepherd," the youth declared, more in pity than in anger, "wherefore do you follow her, like foggy South puffing with wind and rain? You are a thousand times a properer man than she a woman; 'tis such fools as you that make the world full of ill-favoured children; 'tis not her glass, but you that flatters her!" Then he turned again on

Phebe, and, pointing an accusing finger, cried: "But, mistress, know yourself. Down on your knees, and thank heaven, fasting, for a good man's love; for I must tell you friendly in your ear – " He beckoned, and she most willingly left her throne and inclined her head to the youth's red lips as he softly advised, "Sell when you can; you are not for all markets. Cry the man mercy; love him; take his offer!" Then, with a last injunction of Silvius to take his Phebe to himself, the youth and his two companions departed from the glade.

Long after the youth had gone, Phebe sat gazing after him. No youth had ever spoken to her so sternly before; and she was full of bewilderment and sighs. She looked at Silvius, who loved her dearly, and she sighed again. Then she thought of the youth, and her sighs came fast as a blacksmith's bellows. "I'll write to him a very taunting letter," she said thoughtfully, "and thou shalt bear it; wilt thou, Silvius?" she asked, with such a smile at her lover that he, feeling he had been paid in better than gold, could deny her nothing. "I will be bitter with him," she said; and Silvius believed her!

Marching through the forest, with a festive sprig of holly in his cap and whistling an air that was all the fashion with the banished Duke and his companions, Orlando came at last to where the youth and his sister dwelt. "Good day and happiness, dear Rosalind," he announced to his pretended love, with a flourish of his cap and a gallant bow; only to be greeted by a frown, severely folded arms and a tapping of the foot. He was late. "My fair Rosalind," he protested, in answer to her reproaches, "I come within an hour of my promise!"

"Break an hour's promise in love!" cried she; and he, contrite as a crocodile, hung his head and pleaded, "Pardon me, dear Rosalind!" She thought about it; and pardoned him. She was no more able to keep sullen than a child could keep still in church. "Come, woo me, woo me," she commanded, with a royal clap of her hands; "for now I am in a holiday humour, and like enough to consent!" and so once again Celia found herself witness to this strangest of strange courtships in which pretended love hid honest love, and false words were true.

"Am not I your Rosalind?" demanded Rosalind; and Orlando, with a wishful smile, answered, "I take some joy to say you are." Then Rosalind, true to her promise of being contrary, said she would not have him; and he, true to his lover's part, swore it would kill him. But this was too much for Rosalind's good sense. "Men have died from time to time," she said, "and worms have eaten them; but not for love."

He frowned. "I would not have my right Rosalind of this mind," he said, and instantly she changed about. She would indeed have him . . . "And twenty such," she added for good measure.

"What sayest thou?" he cried, outraged. She gazed at him with wide, innocent eyes. "Are you not good?" she asked. He said he hoped he was. "Why then," she declared triumphantly, "can one desire too much of a good thing?" She laughed and turned to Celia. "Come sister, you shall be the priest and marry us!"

Celia stared. Truly, this strange courtship had passed beyond all bounds! "I cannot say the words," she muttered uneasily.

"You must begin," instructed Rosalind, "'Will you Orlando – '" Celia sighed and, shrugging her shoulders, married off the false, yet true, couple who stood hand in hand before her, feeling all the while that a high solemnity was being mocked.

"Now tell me," demanded Rosalind of Orlando after the ceremony was concluded, "how long you would have her after you have possessed her?"

"For ever, and a day," he answered very properly; but she shook her head.

"Say 'a day', without the 'ever'," she advised. "No, no, Orlando; men are April when they woo, December when they wed. Maids are May when they are maids, but the sky changes when they are wives." But Orlando would not believe his Rosalind would ever change, and he put a stop to all arguments that proved the contrary, by remembering that he was to wait upon the Duke at dinner. "For these two hours, Rosalind, I will leave thee."

"Alas! dear love," she cried, clutching him fiercely by the sleeve, "I cannot lack thee two hours!" But there was no help for it; so, after threatening him with her direst displeasure if he should be so much as a minute late in returning, she let him go.

Celia was bursting with indignation over her cousin's outrageous display of female perversity. "You have simply misused our sex in your love-prate!" she cried. "We must have your doublet and hose plucked over your head, and show the world what the bird hath done to her own nest!"

But Rosalind did not care. "O coz, coz, coz," she laughed, flinging out her arms and dancing on the green, "my pretty little coz, that thou didst know how many fathom deep I am in love!" Then, remembering that two long hours must pass, she said, "I'll go find a shadow and sigh till he come."

"And I'll sleep," said Celia, who was not in love.

The two hours came and went, but brought no Orlando. Instead, they wafted another lover through the forest: the breathless Silvius doing his Phebe's bidding. He had brought her letter and faithfully delivered it into Master Ganymede's hand, with humble apologies for the bitter and taunting words that Phebe said she had written. Impatiently, and with many an anxious glance for the coming of Orlando, Rosalind read the letter. Her brow grew dark with anger, and Silvius trembled that his Phebe should have written so cruelly. Rosalind looked up. "Will you hear the letter?" she asked.

"So please you," answered Silvius; so she read it to him. As he listened, his eyes grew big with tears. Phebe had deceived him! The words she had written were bitter, but only to him. The letter he had carried was full of a wild and tender passion; but not for him. She had fallen in love with Ganymede!

"Alas, poor shepherd!" sighed Celia; but Rosalind felt no pity for the foolish youth who was weeping for so worthless a creature as Phebe. "Well, go your way to her, for I see love hath made thee a tame snake!" she cried, angry that love, which should have ennobled, had reduced this lover to so crawling a condition. "Say this to her: if she love me, I charge her to love thee. If she will not, I will never have her – " She stopped. She had glimpsed a familiar figure approaching through the trees. Hastily she dismissed Silvius, and made herself ready for –

But once again, it was not Orlando . . . yet there had been something about the stranger that had, for a moment, deceived her. He was handsome enough (but no Orlando!) and his manner was gentle . . . though inclined to be awkward, like a new garment, not yet worn in. He was looking for a cottage near a clump of olive trees, where a brother and sister dwelt together. As he spoke, he looked curiously at Rosalind and Celia, and wondered if they could be the pair who owned the cottage? "It is no boast, being asked, to say we are," answered Celia; and a sudden summer of roses bloomed in her cheeks as she met the stranger's inquiring gaze.

Nor was the stranger unaffected. He seemed, for a moment, to forget the purpose of his errand. He faltered, looked confused . . . then, recovering himself, began, "Orlando doth commend him to you both – " and at once Rosalind understood why he had reminded her of her love! He had come from Orlando, and therefore bore his imprint! "And to the youth he calls his Rosalind," the stranger continued, "he sends this bloody napkin." He held out a handkerchief, streaked with red.

Rosalind stared at it. "What must we understand by this?" she whispered, suddenly pale. The stranger sighed; then, seating himself cross-legged on the turf, with his audience, like eager children, kneeling before him, he told a story so strange, so wild and wonderful, that the cousins scarcely dared to breathe . . .

It began with Orlando on his way to keep his promise to his imagined Rosalind. As he walked through the forest, full of dreams, he came upon a ragged man, asleep under an ancient tree. About the sleeper's neck, like a lady's bright scarf, was coiled a deadly serpent, which, on hearing Orlando's approach, glided harmlessly away. But a more terrible danger was near at hand. Under a bush crouched a hungry lioness, waiting to leap upon the sleeper with savage teeth and claws! Orlando drew close; then stopped in amazement. He recognized the man! It was his brother, his elder brother Oliver!

"O! I have heard him speak of that same brother," breathed Celia, staring at the stranger as if wondering how he could know so much without having been present himself; "and he did render him the most unnatural that lived amongst men!"

"But to Orlando," cried Rosalind, impatient of brothers and all else, save Orlando. "Did he leave him there – ?"

The stranger shook his head. Though sorely tempted to leave his brother to the lioness, and so be revenged for all the ill-usage he had suffered, he could not do so.

As the lioness roared and sprang, Orlando, without a thought for his own danger, met her in mid-career! They wrestled, and in a moment he had overthrown the savage beast as readily as he had once overthrown the mighty Charles! Here the stranger paused; and then said quietly, "In which hurtling from miserable slumber I awaked!" He himself had been that sleeping man; he was Oliver, Orlando's wicked brother!

The cousins stared at him: Rosalind with anger, but Celia more with sorrow that so fair a young man should turn out to be so black a villain. But no longer! With earnest looks he told them of his most wonderful conversion: of how, having been despatched by the tyrant Duke to bring back Orlando, he had wandered in the forest, becoming more and more wretched until the moment he had awakened from sleep to see Orlando endangering his own life to save his brother's. At once, all envy and malice had vanished from his heart, and now there was only love and forgiveness between himself and Orlando . . .

Celia listened with shining eyes; but Rosalind was still troubled. She had not forgotten the strange token that Orlando had sent. "But, for the bloody napkin?" she asked; and Oliver resumed his story. Orlando had taken him to the banished Duke, where he had been received with great kindness and given fresh clothing; but as Orlando himself was changing his torn attire, he suddenly fainted! The lioness had ripped open his arm, and he had lost much blood. But he quickly recovered and begged Oliver to seek out the brother and sister in the forest to explain to them the reason for his failure to keep his promise. "And," concluded Oliver with a smile, "to give this napkin, dy'd in his blood, unto the shepherd youth that he in sport doth call his Rosalind." He rose, and courteously presented Orlando's crimson gift.

"Why, how now, Ganymede! Sweet Ganymede!"

cried out Celia in a fright; for Rosalind, seeing Orlando's blood, had fainted clean away!

"Many will swoon when they do look on blood," said Oliver; but Celia, vigorously chafing her cousin's cold hands, shook her head. "There is more in it," she muttered. "Cousin! Ganymede!"

Rosalind opened her eyes. "I would I were at home," she murmured; and suffered herself to be helped to her feet. Then, fearful that her sudden weakness had betrayed her sex, she assured Oliver that her fainting had been pretence, that she had not fainted at all, that she had never felt better . . . and that he was to be sure to tell his brother how skilfully she had pretended. She looked to see how well her assurances had been received, and could not help noting some resemblances to Orlando in his elder brother's features: but they were prentice-work compared with what Nature had accomplished when she'd tried again! Celia, on the other hand, as she and Oliver assisted Rosalind back to their cottage, could not help wondering, as she kept glancing at the young man, if Nature, like a lucky player, had not done her best at the first throw! "Good sir," she murmured, as he showed signs of departing, "go with us . . ."

"We shall find a time, Audrey," sighed Touchstone, as the sun went down among the trees, and marriage, like Monday after Sunday, threatened ahead. "Patience, gentle Audrey," he urged as, gazing at his chosen bride ambling foolishly among her goats, he wondered yet again about the wisdom of his choice. But even as he puzzled over it, and would have given much to find some means of delay, there was another in the forest ready to give up all to hasten it!

"My father's house and all the revenue that was old Sir Rowland's will I estate upon you!" cried Oliver distractedly, as he dragged Orlando back to the cottage where Ganymede and his sister Aliena dwelt. He had fallen in love with Aliena, and she with him! It had happened in an instant, in the merest twinkling of eyes; and now, all he desired was to marry Aliena, poor as she was, and live and die by her side, a humble shepherd in the forest.

Orlando marvelled at the swiftness of it all, although why he, who had been struck dumb with love for Rosalind with a suddenness that made his brother's courtship seem almost tedious, should be surprised was a mystery. Nonetheless, he would not stand in their way, and promised to bring the banished Duke and all his followers to celebrate their forest wedding on the morrow. "Go you and prepare Aliena," he advised; "for look you, here comes my Rosalind."

Warmly, Oliver clasped his brother by the uninjured hand; then, greeting the approaching Ganymede as "fair sister", he laughed and hastened to Aliena's cottage.

"O! my dear Orlando," cried Rosalind, regarding his bandages with concern, "how it grieves me to see thee wear thy heart in a scarf!"

"It is my arm!" he protested. She expressed surprise, then inquired if, by any chance, his brother had told him how well she had pretended to faint on seeing his blood?

"Ay," nodded Orlando, "and greater wonders than that," he said, with a smiling look towards the departed Oliver. She took his meaning, and at once confirmed that Aliena's passion was fully the equal of his brother's.

"They are in the very wrath of love," she declared, "they will together: clubs cannot part them!"

"They shall be married tomorrow," Orlando promised; then he sighed, "But O! how bitter a thing it is to look into happiness through another man's eyes!"

"Why then, tomorrow," asked Rosalind softly, "I cannot serve your turn for Rosalind?"

"I can no longer live by thinking," said he.

"I will weary you then no longer with idle talking," said she, much moved by the honesty of Orlando's love and the deepness of his distress. The time was near for truth. Her own heart could scarcely hold out against it. But it must be revealed with proper solemnity and mystery . . . "Believe then, if you please, I can do strange things," she told her lover gravely. "I have, since I was three year old, conversed with a magician . . ." He smiled; but she reproved him with a frown, and continued: "If you do love Rosalind so near the heart as your gesture cries it out, when your brother marries Aliena, shall you marry her."

Orlando stared. "Speakest thou in sober meanings?" he demanded.

"By my life, I do," returned she. "If you will be married tomorrow, you shall; and to Rosalind, if you will . . ."

He would have pressed further, but there were others in the forest who had come to seek out Ganymede. Phebe, the vain and foolish shepherdess, her black eyes screwed up in anger, like rivets in a plank, and with her poor love following after, had come to reproach that youth for reading aloud her very private letter. "You have done me much ungentleness," she complained.

"I care not if I have!" answered Rosalind, wearied by such persistence in folly. "You are there followed by a faithful shepherd; look upon him, love him. He worships you!"

But Phebe shook her silly head. "Tell this youth," she bade the doting Silvius, "what 'tis to love!"

"It is to be all made of sighs and tears," responded Silvius hopelessly; "and so am I for Phebe."

"And I for Ganymede," echoed Phebe, with a yearning look.

"And I for Rosalind," sighed Orlando, adding his link to the chain.

Then all turned to Ganymede, who smiled, and ended the chain most mysteriously with, "And I for no woman!"

Then mystery upon mystery! The strange youth raised a hand and solemnly commanded, "Tomorrow meet me all together;" then spoke to each in turn: first, to Phebe, "I will marry you, if ever I marry woman, and I'll be married tomorrow." Then to Orlando: "I will satisfy you, if ever I satisfied man, and you shall be married tomorrow." And last, to Silvius: "I will content you, if what pleases you contents you, and you shall be married tomorrow!" Then, making a magical sign in the air, doubtless learned from the magician, the youth vanished among the trees, leaving the three lovers to stare and wonder, to hope and doubt if these marvels could ever be brought to pass.

Two little pages from the banished Duke's court, all in green like leaves of holly, with faces bright as berries, came marching through the dawning forest, singing as they went:

> "It was a lover and his lass,
> With a hey, and a ho, and a hey nonino,
> That o'er the green corn-field did pass,
> In spring time, the only pretty ring time,
> When birds do sing, hey ding a ding, ding,
> Sweet lovers love the spring."

As they marched along, keeping time in song and step, all the birds of the forest obliged with a shrill and chattering chorus, from hawthorn, oak and holly . . .

"Dost thou then believe, Orlando," asked the Duke, as he and his followers, with Oliver and his Aliena among them, crowded into the misty chapel of sunshine that was the place appointed for the lovers' meeting, "that the boy can do all this that he hath promised?"

"I sometimes do believe," said Orlando, and then with a sigh, "and sometimes do not." And the little pages went on singing:

"These pretty country folks would lie,
    In spring time, the only pretty ring time . . ."

until suddenly they fell silent as, like a bright phantom passing through the golden pillars of the sun, Ganymede appeared, leading Silvius and Phebe by the hand. Gravely the youth surveyed the assembled congregation, and then addressed the Duke: "If I bring in your Rosalind, you will bestow her on Orlando here?"

"That would I," returned the Duke gladly, "had I kingdoms to give with her!" Ganymede nodded, and turned to Orlando: "And you say you will have her when I bring her?"

"That would I," promised Orlando, "were I of all kingdoms king!" Now was the turn of Phebe. "You say you'll marry me if I be willing?"

"That will I," cried Phebe, all aglow with hope; but Ganymede raised a warning finger. "But if you do refuse to marry me, you'll give yourself to this most faithful shepherd?" Phebe thought; she frowned, she sighed; she looked at Silvius and she smiled. "So is the bargain," she said. Then Ganymede, reminding each and all of their solemn promises, beckoned to Aliena; and, hand in hand, the mysterious brother and sister departed into the forest.

"I do remember in this shepherd boy," frowned the Duke, "some lively touches of my daughter's favour."

Orlando agreed. He too had fancied he'd seen something of Rosalind in Ganymede, and had wondered if he could have been Rosalind's brother. "But my good lord, this boy is forest-born," he began to assure the Duke, when Jacques, his melancholy face crumpling into smiles, announced, "Here comes a pair of very strange beasts, which in all tongues are called fools!"

Sniffing out weddings, like dogs to a dinner, Touchstone and Audrey emerged from among the trees; he, crowned with a chaplet of ivy leaves, and she in her best attire, with her shining happy face poking out from ruff and bonnet, like a festive mutton chop.

"Salutation and greeting to you all!" cried Touchstone grandly, perceiving that he had fallen among courtiers and gentlemen; then, feeling that his choice required some explanation, presented her to the Duke: "A poor virgin, sir, an ill-favoured thing, sir, but mine own: a poor humour of mine, sir, to take that that no man else will." He gave Audrey a shove to indicate that she, in acknowledgement of the tribute paid her, should curtsey gracefully; so down she went, as if to milk her goats. "Bear your body more seeming, Audrey," urged her lord as he engaged in a battle of courtly wits with Jacques; but she could only gape in wonderment as his words, of which she understood not one, flew as fast as fat from a pan. And he, seeing her looks, was well content with his choice: admiration was much to be preferred to equality.

Suddenly, there was a noise in the forest, a strange noise that stilled the birds and hushed the waiting throng. It was a slow, mysterious music, accompanied by solemn drumbeats, like the beating of the forest's heart. A soft breeze began to blow and the air was filled with the scents of spring. The music grew louder and the trees trembled; then the sunbeams seemed to part like golden curtains, making way for a tall, smiling youth in marvellous yellow robes, and bearing a torch. It was Hymen himself, the God of Marriage, who had come to bless the day. Gently, he led by the hand two shining Princesses to complete the fourfold forest wedding, and so bring the promised marvels about!

Amazed and joyful, the Duke recognized in the two Princesses, his daughter and his niece: Oliver, his poor shepherdess Aliena in the Princess Celia, and Orlando, his true love in the one-time Ganymede. "If there be truth in sight," he breathed, "you are my Rosalind!"

"If sight and shape be true," sighed Phebe, no less amazed, but not so joyful to see her Ganymede lost for ever in the fair Rosalind, "why then, my love adieu!" She sighed again, and, turning to the ever-loving Silvius as the better bargain and most true, promised, "I will not eat my word, now thou art mine," and Silvius nearly died of joy!

Then Rosalind united all the lovers' hands, and they knelt for the god to bless their marriages, while the little pages sang:

> "High wedlock then be honoured.
> Honour, high honour and renown,
> To Hymen, god of every town!"

All promises had been kept; but the forest was not yet done with its wonders. The last was still to come. Even as the god departed, and a multitude of joyful explanations broke out, there came a gentleman, flushed with haste and stuffed with news from Duke Frederick's court. That wicked man had taken it into his mad head to set out with a mighty force to seize his brother and put him to death! But no sooner had he come within the charmed circle of the forest than he, like Oliver, had been changed and converted ... not by means of serpent and lioness, but by an old religious man. So powerful had been the words of this venerable person, that the storms that had raged within the unhappy Duke were calmed. He had dismissed his forces, relinquished his crown to his wronged brother, and desired no more than a life of contemplation in the Forest of Arden!

So now all wrongs were righted, and banishment was at an end. The restored Duke turned to his faithful followers and promised: "Every of this happy number that have endured shrewd days and nights with us, shall share the good of our returned fortune!"

At this, there was loud rejoicing, and many a cap was flung into the air. Although in their forest days the courtiers had learned to find, as the wise Duke had once told them, "tongues in trees, books in the running brooks, sermons in stones and good in everything," there was no doubt that soft beds were to be preferred to hard turf, and a sound roof to a leaking sky. The melancholy Jacques alone was of another mind. He, in his time, had seen everything under the tired old sun; and looked only for something new. He chose to remain in the forest, and seek out the company of the changed Duke Frederick: there being more to amuse him in a bad man made good, than in a good man made merely better.

"Stay, Jacques, stay," begged the Duke; but he would not. With a smile and a bow he departed, leaving dancing and merriment behind; and the two little pages singing their hearts out:

"And therefore take the present time,
With a hey, and a ho, and a hey nonino;
For love is crowned with the prime
In spring time, the only pretty ring time,
When birds do sing, hey ding a ding, ding,
Sweet lovers love the spring."

100

Julius Caesar

All Rome was wild with joy! The bright morning streamed with flying caps and pennants, and the very stones danced to the applause of ten thousand feet! Julius Caesar had won a glorious victory over the traitor Pompey, and all the carpenters, cobblers, tradesmen and their wives, shut up shop, put on their best attire, and rushed out of doors to welcome him and crown his statues with garlands, as if he was a king!

"Hence! Home, you idle creatures – "

Two officers of state, high up on the steps of a monument, were shouting furiously to make themselves heard as the noisy crowd came flooding into the market-place, like a filthy, stinking tide, wanting only to lap and lick the feet of Caesar.

"Get you home!"

They drew their swords. The crowd faltered –

"You blocks, you stones, you worse than senseless things!"

Filled with anger and contempt for the common people who, not so long before, had welcomed Pompey even as they now welcomed Caesar, they rushed down and drove them from the market-place, like a frightened flock of sheep. Then, hearing a distant shout of trumpets, they hastened away to clear the streets and uncrown all the stone Caesars they could find.

They were men of the republic. Like the stern marble Romans on their lofty pedestals, who stood on every corner and in every public place, clutching their scrolls of hard-won liberty, they wanted no more crownings and no more kings.

But their task was hopeless. No sooner had they gone, than through a hundred different channels and alleys, the crowd came streaming back, as if the world had tilted Caesar's way. They flowed up steps, they climbed on columns, they clung from windows, as the long brazen trumpets approached, flashing like shooting stars and blasting the air with majesty!

Then came Caesar himself, and suddenly all Rome was one huge adoring eye! Robed in gold and purple, and wearing the laurel wreath of victory, he walked slowly, inclining his head from side to side as he acknowledged the cheering of the people; and the marble Romans on their pedestals seemed to clutch their scrolls more tightly, as if they feared they'd be snatched away.

Following after, like faithful dogs, walked all the great ones of Rome: eager Casca, the noble Brutus with slight Cassius by his side; dry, learned old Cicero, hobbling as if his new sandals pinched, and Mark Antony, stripped and ready to run the course – for it was the Feast of Lupercal when it was the custom for young noblemen to run naked through the streets, striking childless women with leather thongs, to cure them of barrenness.

"Calpurnia!"

The procession halted. The trumpets were stilled. Caesar had spoken. He had summoned his wife. At once she left her place and, almost stumbling over her heavy purple gown in her haste, she came to her husband's side. He bade her stand in Antony's path when he ran the magic course. She was childless and Caesar had need of a son. Humbly, she bowed her head and, accompanied by knowing smiles that made her blush with shame, she returned to her place.

102

"Set on," commanded Caesar. He raised his hand –

"Caesar!"

He paused, and the trumpets, half-way to lips, stayed motionless. Who had called his name? A silence fell on the market-place. Then there was a stirring among the crowd. An old man shuffled forward, a gaunt old man with wild white hair. He was a sooth-sayer who, it was said, looked into tomorrow as clearly as if it was yesterday. He spoke again.

"Beware the Ides of March."

"Set him before me," ordered Caesar; but the old man needed no assistance. Leaning heavily on his staff, he approached and stood before Caesar, his ragged black gown flapping in the gusty air.

"What sayest thou to me now? Speak once again."

"Beware the Ides of March," said the soothsayer, and his words struck a chill into every heart. The Ides of March were close at hand. But Caesar was unmoved. He stared hard into the man's pale blue eyes that blazed either with madness or the harmless folly of age. He smiled.

"He is a dreamer. Let us leave him. Pass." And, with a shrug of his shoulders, as if the warning had been of no more consequence than a pebble cast against the sun, he set on.

Two remained behind: Brutus and Cassius. Wearied of walking in Caesar's shadow, they had no wish to watch him presiding over the Festival games. They leaned against a wall and stared after the swirling clouds of dust that had been raised by the multitude that had streamed after Caesar. Although they were friends they were, at that moment, separate islands of thought. Then Cassius, the quicker and more passion-ate of the two, broke the silence. Shrewdly observing the direction of Brutus's gaze, he wondered if his friend was troubled with the same thought that was troubling himself and certain other gentlemen of Rome? Was it possible, he went on, choosing his words with care, that the noble Brutus, whose great ancestor had driven out the last of Rome's bad kings, was growing uneasy over Caesar's ever-increasing power?

Before Brutus could answer, there came a roar from the distant multitude. "What means this shouting?" he muttered. "I do fear the people choose Caesar for their king!"

"Ay, do you fear it?" asked Cassius quickly. "Then must I think you would not have it so!"

Brutus hesitated; then slowly answered, "I would not . . ." and Cassius's heart beat rapidly. Thus far Brutus was with him!

A cloud passed across the sun. Shadows invaded the market-place. The pale Romans on their pedestals seemed to tremble and sway, as if their ghostly world had begun to shake. They glared down in stony dismay on the two men who murmured together: the one tall and upright, the other, slighter and fiercely restless, like a darting flame striving to set a mighty tree ablaze.

Cassius hated Caesar. He hated him for the huge and arrogant thing he had become.

"Why, man," cried Cassius, seizing his friend by the arm, "he doth bestride the narrow world like a Colossus, and we petty men walk under his huge legs and peep about to find ourselves dishonourable graves!"

At the word 'dishonourable' Brutus flushed angrily. Honour was dearer to him than life itself, and Cassius knew it. Indeed, he loved and admired his friend for it, but such was his hatred for Caesar that he did not scruple to play upon Brutus's honour as if it was an instrument, as he led him further and further along the dangerous path that he himself was treading. And Brutus, to the noble tune of honour, followed the skilful piper willingly.

Caesar was returning. Guiltily, the friends drew apart as the procession entered the market-place. They watched curiously. Plainly, something was amiss. The trumpets hung down like broken daffodils and the crowd had drained away to a ragged trickle. Caesar himself looked angry, and those near him were shaken and pale. They halted. Caesar looked about him, as if for someone on whom he might vent his spleen. His eye fell upon Cassius. He beckoned Mark Antony to his side.

"Let me have men about me that are fat," he said loudly, "sleek-headed men and such as sleep a-nights. Yond Cassius has a lean and hungry look. Such men are dangerous."

"Fear him not, Caesar; he's not dangerous," said Antony with a smile; but Caesar, never taking his eyes from the suddenly white-faced Cassius, slowly shook his head.

"Such men as he be never at heart's ease whiles they behold a greater than themselves," he said thoughtfully, "and therefore are they very dangerous." Then, as if remembering who he was, his hand went to his laurel wreath, which he wore as much to hide his thinning hair as to mark his victory, and settled it more firmly on his head. Others might fear, but never Caesar. "Come to my right hand," he said to Antony, "for this ear is deaf, and tell me truly what thou thinkst of him," and, with a last long look at Cassius, he led the way from the market-place.

As the procession passed, Brutus plucked Casca by the sleeve. Casca, careful not to be observed, lingered behind. Brutus asked him what had happened. Casca looked about him, and, seeing there was none else by, smiled broadly and related what had taken place.

He was full of lively mockery, sparing neither Caesar, nor his friends, nor the people from the sharpness of his tongue; for Casca, though he bowed low before Caesar, was never afraid to speak his mind — behind Caesar's back.

The scene had been so comical and ridiculous that it had been as much as he could do to stop himself laughing aloud. Antony had offered Caesar a crown. Caesar had refused it and the rabble had hooted and shouted for joy. Antony offered it a second time. Again Caesar refused, and again the people cheered him for it. But when it was offered for a third time, and for a third time Caesar pushed it aside, the sweaty crowd yelled and shouted so much that Caesar fell down in a fit and foamed at the mouth — as much from the people's bad breath as from his bitter disappointment that they did not want him to be a king.

"What, did Caesar swoon?" asked Cassius softly.

"'Tis very like," said Brutus; "he hath the falling sickness."

Cassius shook his head. "No, Caesar hath it not; but you, and I, and honest Casca, we have the falling sickness."

Casca looked at him sharply. "I know not what you mean by that," he said; but Cassius had seen in his eyes the very image of his own dark thoughts.

"Will you sup with me tonight, Casca?"

"No, I am promised forth."

"Will you dine with me tomorrow?"

"Ay, if I be alive, and your mind hold, and your dinner worth the eating."

With that, they parted, all three agreeing to meet — tomorrow.

A heap of rags stirred in a dusty corner of the market-place, and, with little groanings and cracklings of the joints, raised itself up to the height of a man. It was the soothsayer. He stared after the three who had just gone; and his pale blue eyes, that looked into tomorrow as clearly as if it was yesterday, widened with dread.

Tomorrow was the Ides of March. The sky darkened and a wind sprang up. Frightened rubbish flew across the market-place, and the old man, his gown stretched out like a black flag, stumbled away.

Then the storm broke, and all Rome shook. It was a strange storm, of sudden enormous glares and enormous blacknesses, and unnatural roarings as if huge lions were rending the sky. Some said blood drizzled on the Capitol, others saw men, all in flames, walking the streets, and dead men shrieking down alleys with their stained winding-sheets streaming out in the dark wind.

"Who's there?"

"A Roman."

Two muffled figures, meeting in a narrow way, drew close together. One was Casca, white with fear at the supernatural violence of the night; the other was Cassius, exulting in it, for he had a storm within as wild as the one above. Fearfully, Casca spoke of monsters in the sky; fiercely Cassius spoke of a monster in Rome –

"'Tis Caesar that you mean, is it not, Cassius?"

"Let it be who it is," muttered Cassius; and, while the earth shook and glaring terrors piled up in the sky, he led the trembling Casca into the darker terror of his own design: the murder of Caesar!

He was not alone, he promised Casca. Even now there were others who had no love for Caesar, waiting in the night. But first they must win Brutus to the cause. The plot had need of him. His noble name would make the deed seem just and honourable in all men's eyes.

"Three parts of him is ours already," whispered Cassius, "and the man entire upon the next encounter . . ." He drew a scroll of paper from his sleeve. It was to be thrown in at Brutus's window. In fiery words it urged him, in the name of the people, to rise up like his great ancestor and rid Rome of the tyrant! Cassius had written it himself. Once more he was playing upon his friend's honour; and this time the tune would lead Brutus to take the final step.

Lightning flashed. The muffled figures shrank back, and their monstrous double shadow was flung across the street like a pall. Then blackness engulfed them . . .

Brutus walked alone in his orchard. The worst of the storm's violence was over, but not its weirdness. Mad shooting stars whizzed across the black sky, breaking up the darkness into a patchwork of flickering sights. At one moment all was hidden and secret; at the next, the clustering trees threw up their thin arms in despair.

"It must be by his death," he whispered as, with an anguished heart, he contemplated the terrible deed that Cassius had put into his thoughts: the killing of a friend, for Caesar *was* his friend. But Caesar's spirit, that huge, ambitious thing that stretched its arm across the world, was the enemy of all free men. "It must be by his death . . ." not because of what he was, but because of what he might become . . .

Someone was coming. It was Lucius, his servant. The boy was puzzled. He'd found a scroll of paper inside the window of his master's room. It had not been there before. Brutus took it, and, when the boy had gone, broke the seal and read:

"Brutus, thou sleep'st. Awake and see thyself! Speak, strike, redress!"

He breathed deeply. It was not the first such letter to reach him. There had been others that had been put in his way. It seemed that all Rome was begging him to act. He clenched up the paper in his fist. Rome should not beg in vain! *"It must be by his death!"*

There was a knocking at the gate. Lucius came to tell him that Cassius was waiting.

"Is he alone?"

"No, sir, there are more with him."

"Do you know them?"

Lucius shook his head. They had all been hidden in their cloaks.

"Let 'em enter," said Brutus, and frowned. Unlike Cassius, he was not a man of plots and conspiracy. He despised concealment and felt ashamed to be a part of it.

Presently, quiet, faceless figures approached from among the trees. One by one, they made themselves known: Casca, Decius, Cinna, Metellus Cimber, Trebonius ... By the light of day, they were men of substance, worthy Romans; but by night, they were something different ... Softly, they talked together while Cassius and Brutus whispered apart. Then Cassius smiled and nodded, and they knew that Brutus was theirs!

He stepped forward and shook each man firmly by the hand, and the bond was sealed. At once, all constraint vanished and they began talking eagerly of what must be done. Brutus was ever in the forefront; his doubts resolved, he embraced the cause with all his heart, and took it upon himself to lead. Should Cicero be approached? His age and dignity would gain all men's respect. But Brutus was against it, and Brutus had his way. Should no one else but Caesar be killed?

"Let Antony and Caesar fall together," said Cassius; but Brutus was against it, and Brutus had his way.

The death of Caesar was to be the sacrifice of a single man for the good of all. "And for Mark Antony," he said, "think not of him, for he can do no more than Caesar's arm when Caesar's head is off."

"Yet I fear him," muttered Cassius; but he was overruled.

The hour was late. It was three o'clock in the morning, and the heavy blackness was already wearing thin.

"Good gentlemen," urged Brutus, as his companions, with pale and desperate looks, took their leave, "look fresh and merrily ..." but when they had gone, the show of ease he had put on, left him, and once more he was the lonely brooding figure among the trees. "It must be by his death ..." They were to meet at Caesar's house at eight o'clock to bring him to the Capitol, and there to kill him –

"Brutus, my lord."

He started. Portia, his wife, stood beside him, like a good spirit in the ugly dark. She was troubled. She had seen the secret men in the orchard, and she knew her husband was distressed. Gently, she begged him to tell her the cause.

He turned away. He dared not tell her. He feared her honesty too much.

"I am not well in health," he said, "and that is all."

Angered at being put off with thin excuses, as if she had no more understanding than a child, she reproached him for his lack of trust. Were he and she not one? Why, then, should she not share in his griefs as well as in his joys?

"Am I your self," she demanded, confronting him wherever he turned, "in sort or limitation, to keep with you at meals, comfort your bed, and talk to you sometimes? Dwell I but in the suburbs of your good pleasure? If it were no more, then Portia is Brutus' harlot, not his wife!" In despair, she knelt. "Tell me your counsels," she pleaded, "I will not disclose 'em!"

Eagerly, she dragged up her gown and displayed a deep and bloody wound in her white thigh. She herself

110

had done it and endured the pain in silence as a proof of her fortitude.

"Can I bear that with patience, and not my husband's secrets?"

"O ye gods," wept Brutus, shamed by Portia's courage, "render me worthy of this noble wife!" and, with a warm embrace, promised that she should share in the terrible secret he carried in his heart.

"Help, ho, they murder Caesar!"

But it was only in the dreams of Caesar's wife. She awoke with a cry. She left her bed and rushed in search of her husband. She found him already preparing himself to go to the Capitol. Urgently, she begged him to stay at home that day. Not only had her dreams been full of blood, but all night the sky had roared and glared with fiery doom. But Caesar only smiled and shook his head.

"These predictions are to the world in general as to Caesar."

"When beggars die there are no comets seen," cried Calpurnia, "the heavens themselves blaze forth the death of princes!"

Caesar was unmoved. Neither the savage sights in the streets nor the dreadful portents in the sky could shake him. He was always Caesar.

"Alas, my lord," pleaded Calpurnia, her fears increasing a thousandfold as a troubled servant came to tell that the morning's sacrifice had been unlucky: no heart had been found in the slaughtered beast, "do not go forth today!"

She knelt and, weeping, implored him to send Mark Antony to say he was not well and would not come to the Capitol today.

Caesar gazed down. A single word from him would turn Calpurnia's trembling fear to boundless joy. He raised her to her feet.

"Mark Antony shall say I am not well," he said; but even as Calpurnia burst into sunshine smiles, a gentleman arrived, a gentleman whose looks were fresh and merry. It was Decius. It was eight o'clock and he had come to take Caesar to the Capitol.

"Bear my greeting to the senators," said Caesar, "and tell them I will not come today."

Decius stared, and the freshness seemed to wither on his cheeks.

"Say he is sick," said Calpurnia quickly.

Caesar frowned. "Shall Caesar send a lie? Go tell them Caesar will not come."

"Most mighty Caesar," pleaded Decius, plainly distressed, "let me know some cause – "

"The cause is in my will. I will not come. That is enough to satisfy the Senate." Then, taking pity on the bewildered Decius, he explained that Calpurnia had begged him, on her knees, to stay at home. She had had bad dreams. She had dreamed that Caesar's statue had spouted blood, and that smiling Romans had come to bathe their hands in it.

Decius, clever Decius, listened carefully. He shook his head. Calpurnia had interpreted her dream quite wrongly. Its true meaning was life, not death. The spouting blood plainly signified the nourishment that Caesar was to give to Rome. Caesar nodded thoughtfully. He picked up his laurel wreath and absently fingered the leaves as Decius went on to say that he'd heard the Senate meant to offer Caesar the crown that very day; but if Caesar did not come, Decius feared they'd change their minds and even whisper that Caesar had been frightened by his wife's dreams.

Caesar's brow grew dark. "Give me my robe," he commanded, outraged that a pack of feeble old men should dare to think Caesar afraid. "I will go!"

Calpurnia cried out in dismay; but her voice was

lost and she was brushed aside and forgotten as the room was suddenly filled with smiling friends who had come to drink wine with Caesar, and then to take him to the Capitol and his death.

They were betrayed! A man stood in the crowd outside the Capitol, with a letter for Caesar in his hand. In it, the conspiracy was revealed and every guilty name written down! There was a sound of cheering from afar. Caesar was coming! Trembling with excitement, the man began to push his way towards the front . . .

Portia in her house also heard the cheering, but to her distracted ears it sounded ragged and dismayed. Every noise from the Capitol excited her, every silence drove her mad. A dozen times she'd bade Lucius run to the Senate House; but still he stayed, for she could think of no likely reason for his errand. Her husband's secret struggled in her breast, and it needed all her strength to keep it confined.

"O Brutus," she whispered, "the heavens speed thee in thine enterprise!" and once more she bade Lucius run to her husband, for no better purpose than to tell him she was merry!

The sun glared down after the night's storm, as if to see where all the monsters had gone. It was past nine o'clock and Caesar, walking in the midst of his friends, approached the Capitol. He paused. He had spied a face that he remembered among the waiting crowds. It was the mad old man who had spoken to him yesterday. He beckoned and the old man came forward, leaning on his staff.

"The Ides of March are come," said Caesar mockingly.

"Ay, Caesar," answered the soothsayer, "but not gone."

Caesar laughed, and passed on.

113

"Hail, Caesar! Read this – "

A man had rushed out of the crowd and, before anyone could stop him, had thrust a letter into Caesar's hand! Swiftly Decius interposed with a letter of his own for Caesar to read.

"O Caesar, read mine first," begged the man, "for mine's a suit that touches Caesar nearer!"

"What touches us ourself shall be last served," said Caesar royally; and thrust the fatal letter into the oblivion of his sleeve.

"Delay not, Caesar," cried the man, "read it instantly!"

"What, is the fellow mad?" demanded Caesar; and Cassius bustled him back into the crowd.

Then, with a last smile and wave to the people of Rome, Caesar mounted up the steps of the Capitol and disappeared within. 'Caesar, beware of Brutus. Take heed of Cassius. Come not near Casca . . .' warned the letter in his sleeve; but in vain.

Trebonius was deep in talk with Mark Antony, and was gently leading him away. It had been agreed. Caesar's was the only blood to be shed. There was to be no frantic butchery. It was to be done swiftly and sternly, in a spirit of Justice, not revenge.

Casca was to strike the first blow. With his right hand hidden in his gown, he walked as if on egg-shells, and sweated like an actor fearful of mangling his part. Every sight, every sound was betrayal – the echoing footsteps on the huge marble floor, the murmuring of senators as they moved among the tall shadowy columns to take their places in the solemn circle of chairs; the quick glances, the sudden silences . . . Cassius was pale, anxious; his eyes were burning as if his brain was on fire. But Brutus, as always, was upright and calm . . .

Suddenly there was a stirring. The senators were

standing. What had happened? What had they seen? But it was for Caesar. He had taken his place in the chair of state. He motioned graciously with his hand and the senators seated themselves again. They leaned forward, like an expectant audience at the beginning of a play.

It was to begin with Metellus Cimber. Casca moved quietly to the back of Caesar's chair. He waited. Metellus had not moved. He had been forestalled. Someone else was addressing Caesar, and speaking at length. Metellus was rubbing his hands together, as if to wipe off the skin. At last it was his turn. Quickly he came forward and knelt before Caesar and began to plead for the pardon of his banished brother. Coldly, Caesar denied him. Then Brutus came forward, then Cassius, then Cinna ... until all were kneeling, pleading:

"Most high, most mighty ... Pardon, Caesar, pardon ... O Caesar ..."

But Caesar was unmoved.

Casca stood directly behind. His heart was knocking violently. Of a sudden, the man seated in the chair seemed immense! He towered above the crouching figures before him like a god! Cinna had clutched the hem of his robe, in abject supplication. Caesar spurned him.

"Great Caesar – " cried Decius; and Casca's hidden hand was out!

"Speak," he screamed, "hands for me!" and, reaching forward, plunged his dagger into Caesar's neck!

Caesar cried out! He clapped his hand to his wound as if an insect had stung him. He rose to his feet, turned, seized Casca by the wrist – But Casca's cry had been answered! The kneeling figures were up, their arms were lifted, and in every hand was a weapon!

115

Amazed, Caesar stared from face to terrible face. He knew them all. They were his friends . . .

Then they fell upon him. With gasps and cries and savage grunts, they stabbed and slashed and hacked where they could, driving him this way and that, until Caesar was no more than a swaying, staggering remnant, everywhere spouting blood. But still he would not die; until Brutus, with a sad look, struck the last blow.

"Et tu, Brute?" he sighed as his friend's dagger pierced him through. "Then fall Caesar!" and with his ruined face muffled in his slashed gown, he fell at the base of Pompey's statue. Caesar was dead.

There was silence. It was as if the heart of the world had been torn out, leaving an emptiness. Then Cinna cried out:

"Liberty! Freedom! Tyranny is dead!" and the world awoke!

There was an uproar of overturned chairs and stumbling feet as terrified senators, squealing like chickens rushing from the axe, fled from the men of blood.

"Fly not, stand still!" shouted Brutus. "Ambition's debt is paid!" but the senators, seeing only wild-eyed murderers and streaming knives, stumbled out of doors, leaving behind one old man, grey-faced and trembling, who had been too frightened to move.

"There's no harm intended to your person," Brutus assured him; and Cassius led him gently away.

The conspirators were alone. They stared down at the fallen Caesar. The hugeness of their deed filled them with awe and robbed them of all thought and action. Then Brutus proposed they should stoop and bathe their hands, ceremonially, in Caesar's blood, to sanctify what they had done.

"How many ages hence," murmured Cassius, as his kneeling friends, some boldly, some fearfully, fumbled in the dead man's wounds, "shall this our lofty scene be acted over in states unborn and accents yet unknown?" and he gazed round at the wrenched and broken circle of empty chairs, as if the countless generations to come were already crowding in and looking on.

"How many times shall Caesar bleed in sport?" wondered Brutus.

"So oft as that shall be," said Cassius proudly, "so often shall the knot of us be called the men that gave their country liberty!"

A shadow fell across them. There was a figure standing in the open doorway. It was a servant of Mark Antony. He came quickly forward and knelt to Brutus. His master had sent him. Antony asked for no more than safe conduct to come before Brutus; and, if Brutus should satisfy him that Caesar's death had been necessary, he would be content to follow where the noble Brutus led.

"He shall be satisfied," said Brutus, and sent the servant back. It would be well to have Mark Antony for a friend.

"I wish we may," said Cassius quietly. "But yet I have a mind that fears him much."

Mark Antony came directly. His eyes were still looped with shadows from a long night's drinking and his step was unsteady; for he was a lover of wine and good company. Then he saw Caesar, huddled in his torn and bloody gown, like a dead beast roughly covered over, to keep the flies away. He stopped, and tears filled his eyes.

"O mighty Caesar! Dost thou lie so low?" he wept helplessly. "Fare thee well!"

He was a young man of quick, strong feelings which, try as he might, he could not hide. His heart was breaking, for he had loved and admired Caesar above all other men. He turned to Brutus and his friends and begged them, if they bore him any ill-will, to kill

117

him there and then, with the very weapons with which they had killed Caesar.

"O Antony," protested Brutus, much moved by the young man's grief, "beg not your death of us!" and he promised that, when the frightened people had been calmed, he would satisfy him with good reasons for Caesar's death.

Antony nodded; and, on a sudden impulse that was the mark of his nature, he shook each man by his bloody hand, as if to enrol himself among the givers of liberty. Brutus's wish was gratified. Mark Antony was their friend. All he asked in return, was leave to speak at Caesar's funeral. A small request.

"You shall, Mark Antony," said Brutus warmly.

"Brutus, a word with you!"

It was Cassius. He beckoned Brutus away.

"You know not what you do," he warned. "Do not consent!"

He did not trust Mark Antony and feared what he might say. But Brutus brushed his fears aside. He had foreseen that danger and was prepared. Antony would speak only after he himself had addressed the people and given them the reason for Caesar's death. He was not to blame Brutus and his companions, nor was he to say more in praise of Caesar than was proper for a friend. If Antony did not agree to these conditions, he was not to speak at all.

"Be it so," murmured Antony when Brutus told him. "I do desire no more."

"Prepare the body, then, and follow us," said Brutus; and, with a reassuring smile at the still troubled Cassius, led the way outside to face the people of Rome.

Antony was alone in the silent building. Around him, the pale columns grew upward, losing themselves in shadows; and on the floor, like the track of a hunted deer, were smears and spots and puddles of blood.

Antony knelt. With trembling hands he uncovered Caesar's face. He stared at it long and hard, as if to engrave each savage wound upon his memory for ever. Then he looked up; and with eyes that blazed with grief and rage, he vowed so terrible a revenge for the foul crime that all Italy would bleed for it!

The news of Caesar's death rushed through the city like a wind, whipping up excitement, fear and bewilderment. The great man, the fixed star that had held all in place, was gone! The world was in darkness, even at noon!

But to Brutus, the world was already a brighter and a nobler place now that the danger of Caesar's ambition had been cut off. He stood on the steps of the Capitol with all Rome crowding to hear him.

"Romans, countrymen, and lovers," he shouted, striving to calm the huge tide of people that rose and fell before him like an unruly sea, "hear me for my cause!"

He told them why Caesar had been killed; and they cheered. He told them they were free; and they cheered. He told them they were proud Romans, and they cheered till the very air was dazed; not for what he said, but because he was the noble Brutus who would tell them what to do. Then, when Mark Antony appeared, with two servants bearing Caesar's sheeted body, which they laid upon a hastily prepared bier, he waved his dagger, still bright with Caesar's blood, over his head and cried that even as he had killed Caesar for the good of Rome, he would kill himself if Rome should ever need his death!

"Live, Brutus, live, live!" roared the crowd. "Let him be Caesar!"

Brutus stared at them, amazed. Was it possible that

they wanted another tyrant so soon after they had been saved from one?

"My countrymen – " he pleaded, but they would not listen; and he was compelled to beg them, over and over again, to stay and hear Mark Antony before they let him depart, with "Let him be Caesar!" still ringing in his ears.

Brutus and the conspirators had gone. Antony was alone before the people of Rome. He came forward. The crowd stirred impatiently. After the success of Brutus, Antony was a slight figure on the steps. He began to speak, humbly. He said he spoke by permission of Brutus and his friends; but the crowd, catching only the name, angrily warned him to speak no ill of the noble Brutus. Antony bowed his head.

"You gentle Romans – " he began again; but the crowd was still restless. Suddenly he took a step towards Caesar's bier. The dead man's arm had slipped from the shroud and was hanging down, like butcher's meat. Quickly, Antony took it up, and, kissing the half-clenched hand, laid it across Caesar's breast. It was simply done, and with perfect naturalness; but, like the artless gesture of a skilful actor, it caught every eye.

"Friends, Romans, countrymen," he shouted, in a voice that shook the very stones of Rome, "lend me your ears!"

But there was no need. He had already seized attention by the throat; and he held it fast! The vast crowd stood motionless; wives turned from their husbands, young men from their loves, and even the ever-running children stopped, stared, and listened as Mark Antony spoke of the dead.

Cautiously at first, and ever-mindful of the need to please his hearers with praise for Brutus, he began to conjure up the Caesar they had lost: a Caesar men might weep for, a Caesar who was good and just; a

Caesar whose only ambition was for his country, and in whose mighty heart there was room enough for love of every soul in Rome.

He spoke as a simple, honest man to simple, honest men. As Cassius had feared, he spoke not to their reason, but to their feelings –

"Bear with me," he cried, his eyes fiery with tears, "my heart is in the coffin there with Caesar, and I must pause till it come back to me!"

A murmuring of pity sprang up, ruffling through the crowd and shivering it, like a sudden change of wind. Swiftly, he began to work upon it, until the shivering became a heaving and swelling, like the breathing of a giant beast. He showed the people a parchment. It was Caesar's will. The crowd pressed forward. Antony drew back. It was wrong for the people to know that their Caesar had loved them so well that he had made them all his heirs. It might turn them against the 'honourable men' who had stabbed Caesar to death!

"They were villains, murderers!" shouted the crowd, enraged with grief and greed. "The will! Read the will!"

But still Antony held off, knowing that each time he dammed the ever-increasing tide it would gather in strength.

"If you have tears, prepare to shed them now!" he cried, and held up, for all to see, Caesar's robe, torn and bloody from dagger thrusts, as if wild beasts had been rending it; and then, with one fierce movement, he snatched away the shroud and showed the people Caesar himself, the man who had loved them, hacked and mangled by his friends!

Only then, when the people's fury had mounted to its utmost pitch, did he read the will. For every man, a sum of money, and Caesar's orchards and gardens and walks had been left to the people for them to enjoy for ever!

"Here was a Caesar!" shouted Antony, as the crowd

roared and howled for vengeance on the cruel murderers. "When comes such another?"

"Never, never!" came the huge reply; and there was scarcely time for Antony to cover the body for decency's sake, before, like a bloody banner, it was borne triumphantly aloft!

"Mischief, thou art afoot," whispered Antony as he hastened away. "Take thou what course thou wilt!" and the maddened multitude, like a monstrously swollen river, burst its banks!

It rushed through the city, smashing windows, tearing out the frames and sweeping all to destruction in its path, with the dead Caesar, like a piece of wreckage on a raging tide, tossed this way and that, now down, now bolt-upright and grinning horribly at his revenge!

There was a man walking peaceably in a street. He was a quiet, humble fellow, a poet, a dreamer of sweet dreams, who had never done the world any harm. Suddenly the crowd came upon him. Fiercely, they demanded his name. By ill-luck, it was Cinna –

"Tear him to pieces!" screamed the crowd. "He's a conspirator!"

"I am Cinna the poet! I am Cinna the poet!" pleaded the poor wretch; but his name was still Cinna so they tore him, shrieking, limb from limb. Tyranny was dead; and so was Cinna the poet.

Then with howls and yells and blazing brands, the crowd, more terrible by far than the wild apparitions that had stalked the streets in the prophetic storm, rushed away to wreak its vengeance on the conspirators!

In Mark Antony's house, three men sat at a table that was coldly laid for death. One was Antony himself; another was Lepidus, a sturdy soldier with valuable legions at his command; the third was a pale, precise young man, younger, even, than Antony, who glanced with thin-lipped disapproval at the empty bottles and faded remembrances of ladies that littered the room. He was Octavius, grand-nephew of Caesar and heir to his mighty name.

"Prick him down, Antony," he murmured, nodding towards a list of names that lay upon the table between them.

Antony looked down and, with a careless stroke of his pen, condemned yet another man to death. Not for such men as these was there the foolish magnanimity of a Brutus who had once spared Antony's life! It needed but the faintest shadow cast on a man's loyalty for him to be dragged from his bed, his throat cut, and his possessions seized.

It was a dangerous time. The murder of Caesar had split the land and unleashed the terror of war. Brutus and Cassius had fled from the wrath of the people and were, even now, gathering armies beyond Rome. More and more money was wanted for soldiers to march against them. With a wave of his hand, Antony despatched Lepidus to Caesar's house to fetch his will. The promised legacies would have to be cut off. Everything was needed to pay for the war.

"This is a slight unmeritable man," said Antony contemptuously, when Lepidus had gone; and he proposed that, once the fellow had served his turn, he and Octavius should rid themselves of him.

"But he's a tried and valiant soldier," protested Octavius.

"So is my horse," said Antony.

Octavius let it pass. He had no wish to quarrel with Antony. Young as he was, he was already politician enough to know better than to mingle feelings with policy. Nothing must be allowed to deflect them from their chief purpose, which was the destruction of Brutus and Cassius and all who had inclined to them. He stood up, and, looking over Antony's shoulder, observed with cold satisfaction that the list of names was black with spots of death.

Brutus, encamped near Sardis in far-off Asia Minor, also needed money for war. He had sent to Cassius; but had been denied. Now, with his huge army stretched out across the fields like a monstrous harvest of steel, waving and glinting as far as the eye could see in the setting sun, he waited outside his tent for some explanation from his friend.

His old calmness had forsaken him. His heart, already heavy with bad news from home, had been stirred to anger by Cassius's doubtful behaviour, not only in denying him money, but because he had dared to plead for a man that he, Brutus, had punished for taking bribes. Even in war, their hands must be clean and their hearts unspotted.

"Most noble brother, you have done me wrong!" were Cassius's first words when they met, and spoken loud.

He had come with his officers, ahead of his marching legions, and now confronted Brutus. He, too, was an angry man; and, unlike his friend, made no effort to hide it. He had not liked the manner in which Brutus had reproached him for seeking to defend his guilty officer. He stood, breathing deeply, his brow dark and his fists clenched; and saw himself reflected, Medusa-like, in Brutus's too-bright breastplate: a frowning fellow in armour that was worn and soiled from hard fighting, very like the man himself.

Quietly, Brutus bade him come inside his tent. It was not wise for discord between generals to be in the public gaze. Accordingly, they dismissed their officers and, with an outward show of harmony, retired into Brutus's tent. But once the heavy, dim interior had enclosed them and shut them away from curious eyes, the division between them sprang wide apart.

The cause was money: money denied, and money got

from bribery, which Brutus hated and despised. Private grief and the multiplying troubles of war had so stiffened his pride and encased him in the armour of his honour, that he could not forgive even the smallest falling away from honesty, least of all when he saw it in his friend.

"Let me tell you, Cassius," he said, as if to an underling, "you yourself are much condemned to have an itching palm . . ."

"I an itching palm!" cried Cassius, unable to believe that Brutus could address him so contemptuously.

"Remember March, the Ides of March remember. Did not great Julius bleed for justice' sake?" went on Brutus, as if careless of the deep hurt he had inflicted. "Shall we now contaminate our fingers with base bribes? . . . I had rather be a dog and bay the moon, than such a Roman."

"Brutus, bait not me," Cassius pleaded, striving with all his might to control his outraged heart. "You forget yourself. I am a soldier, I, older in practice, abler than yourself to make conditions!"

"Go on! You are not, Cassius."

"I am."

"I say you are not."

"Urge me no more!" warned Cassius, his hand going helplessly to his sword. "Have mind upon your health!"

"Away, slight man!" jeered Brutus; and, while Cassius spent himself in useless rage, he pricked and stabbed and hacked him with words as cold and sharp as steel, never giving him rest, ever accusing, ever condemning, until Cassius, staggering even as Caesar had staggered under the dagger-thrusts, could endure no more.

"Come, Antony, and young Octavius, come," he wept, sinking to his knees, "revenge yourselves alone on Cassius, for Cassius is aweary of the world . . ." He drew his dagger and offered it to Brutus. "Strike as

125

thou didst at Caesar," he begged; "for I know, when thou didst hate him worst, thou lov'dst him better than ever thou lov'dst Cassius."

They stared at one another, these two friends who had come so far together since the Ides of March, and marvelled that it should have come to this: that one should now be begging his death of the other.

"Sheathe your dagger," muttered Brutus, suddenly ashamed; and, with an effort, thrust aside his private sorrow and confessed that he had been ill-tempered.

At once, Cassius, as quick to forgive as he was in everything, smiled. "Give me your hand!" he cried.

"And my heart too," answered Brutus gladly; and their hands were clasped once more in friendship. He called for his servant Lucius to bring a bowl of wine.

"I did not think you could have been so angry," murmured Cassius, as they waited.

"O Cassius," sighed Brutus, "I am sick of many griefs;" and then, unable any longer to hide the aching desolation in his heart, he told Cassius that Portia was dead.

Cassius drew in his breath sharply. "How 'scaped I killing when I crossed you so?" he whispered, in a rush of pity for his friend. "O insupportable and touching loss! Upon what sickness?"

No sickness but fear: fear for her husband, and fear of Antony and Octavius's growing strength. She had killed herself.

"Speak no more of her," pleaded Brutus, as Lucius came in with wine and with lighted tapers that changed the dark tent into a solemn golden cave.

The friends drank. There was a sound of voices outside. Lucius departed and a moment later, brought in two officers, Messala and Titinius. Brutus bade them be seated . . .

"Portia," sighed Cassius, his thoughts still with the

lively lady whose dear love and sweet honesty had lightened Brutus's life, "art thou gone?"

"No more, I pray you!" whispered Brutus urgently; and, turning to the officers was, in a moment, his calm, unshaken self.

He had letters from Rome. Mark Antony and Octavius, with their armies, were marching towards Philippi. Messala nodded. He also had had letters confirming it. In addition, he had heard that a hundred senators had been put to death. Brutus had heard the same.

"Had you your letters from your wife, my lord?" asked Messala gently.

Brutus shook his head. Messala asked if his letters had contained any news of his wife? Again Brutus shook his head. Messala glanced quickly at Titinius, and in that glance it was plain that he knew of Portia's death and dreaded telling Brutus of it. Cassius scowled and turned away. His heart ached for his friend.

"Then like a Roman bear the truth I tell," said Messala steadily, "for certain she is dead . . ."

Brutus bowed his head. "Why, farewell, Portia," he murmured, and Messala and Titinius marvelled at his fortitude; but Cassius knew that such fortitude was paid for with a sea of inward tears.

"Well, to our work," said Brutus, abruptly dismissing all grief for the immediate necessity. "What do you think of marching to Philippi presently?"

Cassius was against it. It was wiser, he reasoned, for the enemy to come to them, and so waste himself with journeying. But Brutus knew better. The enemy was more likely to gain in strength from marching through a friendly countryside, whereas they themselves were already at the height of their power and could only decline.

"There is a tide in the affairs of men," he said, "which, taken at the flood, leads on to fortune; omitted, all the voyage of their life is bound in shallows and miseries." He paused; then went on: "We must take the current when it serves, or lose our ventures."

There was silence. Then one by one, his companions, their faces glowing in the tapers' yellow light, nodded. It was agreed. Tomorrow they were to set out for Philippi and the battle that would decide their fates. Quietly they took their leave.

Presently Brutus was alone. All but one of the tapers had been extinguished and the camp was quiet; but he could not sleep. He called for Lucius to play some music to him. The boy came, stumbling and clutching his lute, still half in his dreams.

"This is a sleepy tune," smiled Brutus as the music began. Then it ceased; the boy was fast asleep. Brutus gazed at him, enviously; but did not wake him. Gently he took the instrument from his hands and put it aside, lest it break in falling to the floor. He drew his seat close to the taper and tried to read; but the flame was sickly: it shook and trembled like a fevered spirit.

"How ill this taper burns!" he muttered, and laid his book aside.

The sleeping boy was smiling; he was in a happier time. Brutus sighed, and gazed into the crowding shadows that shifted, like uneasy thoughts, in the quiet tent. Smoke from the taper weaved up into the air, where it hovered curiously, as if it had met with an invisible obstruction. As he watched, it seemed to grow pale and form itself into the shape of a robe.

Drops of sweat gathered on Brutus's brow as, little by little, the robe became inhabited, and flowers of blood began to blossom amid the folds.

"Ha! Who comes here?" he whispered, as if to deny the fearful evidence of his senses.

"Thy evil spirit, Brutus," answered the apparition, fixing him with a pallid stare. It was Caesar, torn and bloody in his murder gown, even as Brutus had seen him when he'd stabbed him to death.

"Why com'st thou?"

"To tell thee thou shalt see me at Philippi."

"Well; then I shall see thee again?"

"Ay, at Philippi," came the solemn answer; and, with a gesture of farewell, the ghost of murdered Caesar faded and dissolved into the air.

The plains of Philippi swarmed with armed men, thick as bees.

"Mark Antony, shall we give sign of battle?" asked Octavius eagerly, his thin blood suddenly heated to a youthful rashness as a little group of horsemen, their breastplates glittering, came rapidly towards them, under the scarlet banner of war.

Antony, the seasoned soldier, smiled contemptuously, and shook his head.

"No, Caesar," he said, as Brutus and Cassius and their officers drew near, "the generals would have some words."

Presently they were face to face: the mighty enemies whose quarrel had divided the world. They stared at one another, silently noting the change that had been wrought by time and struggle; how much older and harsher they all looked, like men of rough-hewn stone! Their meeting was brief and bitter. Antony savagely denounced the murderers of Caesar, and they flung back his words with angry scorn.

"A peevish schoolboy," jeered Cassius, "joined with a masker and a reveller!"

"Old Cassius still!" mocked Antony, yet with an unwilling affection for the man of passion who, in some ways, was more his fellow than was the bloodless youth by his side.

"Come, Antony," cried Octavius, wearied of insults and impatient for deeds, "away!" And so they parted, returning to their waiting legions, to make ready for the coming battle that for many would be their last.

"Messala," called Cassius, while Brutus was conferring apart with another of his officers.

Messala came to his side. Cassius smiled; but there was no pleasure in it. It was the saddened smile of a man suddenly tired of the fury of life. "This is my birthday," he confided; and, as Messala shook him by the hand, he charged him to bear witness that he had been compelled, against his better judgement, to risk all on the outcome of a single battle. He had strong forebodings of disaster.

"Believe not so," urged Messala; and Cassius, for a brief while, put on a cheerful face; but when he spoke with Brutus, it was of what should be done if the battle was lost, and how they should end their lives.

There was a grave solemnity between the friends as they spoke together. "This same day," said Brutus quietly, "must end that work the Ides of March begun, and whether we shall meet again I know not. Therefore our everlasting farewell take." He held out his hand, and Cassius took it firmly in his own. "For ever, and for ever, farewell, Cassius. If we do meet again, why, we shall smile; if not, why then this parting was well made."

"For ever, and for ever, farewell, Brutus," said Cassius, with a long and steady look. "If we do meet again, we'll smile indeed; if not, 'tis true this parting was well made."

Then they turned, and, with a last wave of the hand in a last farewell, rode away, each to his own command.

The bright morning grew still, as if, for a moment, all Nature was holding its breath. Then, with a sudden scream of trumpets and a roaring of drums, the legions began to move. As they did so, a vast cloud of dust rose up from the plain, and the earth shook under the tread of the opposing armies, like the mighty heart-beat of the world.

Now more clouds, tossed with pennants and pricked with sharp glints of steel, began to roll and billow down from the hills until, with a thunderous uproar, all met together like rushing waters, tumbling down, one upon another.

All day long the battle raged, with ever-changing fortunes, now inclining this way, now that, until the very sun was steeped in blood, and sank, dying, below the hills.

At last it was over, and a thankful darkness over-spread the field, turning those who had died in triumph and those who had fallen in defeat, all alike into quiet black shapes. A single torch, like a flaring moth, wandered hither and thither, sometimes hovering to illumine upturned faces, like pale streaked flowers; then it moved on, with a little group of men wearily following after.

"Come, poor remains of friends," sighed Brutus, "rest on this rock."

They halted, and, with heavy looks and aching hearts, sank down, some sitting with dazed head falling forward onto huddled knees, some leaning back against the rock and staring up at the cold stars. Brutus alone remained standing, sword in hand, as if to kill a ghost.

All was lost. Antony and Octavius had won the day. Cassius was dead. Rather than be taken by the enemy, he had killed himself with the very weapon that had stabbed Caesar.

"O Julius Caesar, thou art mighty yet," Brutus had wept when he'd looked down on the still face of his friend, whose eager fire was out, "thy spirit walks abroad and turns our swords in our own proper entrails."

Softly Brutus called to one of the pitiful few who seemed to cling about the rock like the sea-torn remnants of a wreck. The man came and Brutus whispered an urgent request. The man stared at him in dread. He shook his head and shrank away.

"What ill request did Brutus make of thee?" asked one of his companions.

"To kill him . . ."

Now Brutus summoned another, and made the same terrible request. But the man would not; and the third he asked, answered:

"That's not an office for a friend, my lord."

Suddenly there was heard a distant trumpet and a sound of shouting. Hastily, the friends arose . . . all save one who had been fast asleep: a fellow by the name of Strato, a thick-necked, sturdy fellow with an honest, albeit sleepy face.

Urgently, they begged Brutus to fly. He promised that he would; and, as his friends left him, he laid a hand on Strato's arm and asked him to stay behind. Strato, as slow to leave a friend in need as he was to save himself, stayed by Brutus's side.

"Thy life," said Brutus, to this last companion, "hath had some smatch of honour in it. Hold then my sword, and turn away thy face, while I do run upon it. Wilt thou, Strato?"

Strato, dull of wit but stout of heart, did not like the office; but he knew there was no other way. He was not a thinker, as Brutus was; but, like Brutus, he counted honour above mere life.

"Give me your hand first," he demanded; and, as Brutus clasped his hand, he took the sword and held it firmly. "Fare you well, my lord," he murmured, and turned away his face.

"Farewell, good Strato," whispered Brutus; and, with a last sad look about him, sighed: "Caesar, now be still. I killed not thee with half so good a will!"

132

Then, with one swift movement, he ran upon the sword; and, as the sharp steel entered him, his life rushed gladly out.

Gently, Strato withdrew the sword and laid it by his master's side. Then he arranged the body so that it should lie decently; and stood beside it to tell the world that Brutus had died as he had lived, with courage and with honour.

He was still there, the solitary sentinel, when the victors, their triumphant faces glowing in torchlight as they searched the battlefield for the chief of their enemies, at last came upon Brutus, dead.

"I held the sword," Strato told them proudly, "and he did run on it."

Mark Antony nodded. He understood such a death, even if he did not understand such a life.

"This was the noblest Roman of them all," he said, gazing down with respect upon the calm, proud face of his enemy, the man who had committed the worst of deeds for the best of reasons. "His life was gentle, and the elements so mixed in him, that Nature might stand up and say to all the world, 'This was a man!'"

Even as he said it, he glanced sideways at the cold, precise young man, who stood beside him; and slightly shook his head.

"According to his virtue let us use him," said Octavius, impatient to have done with wasteful generosity to the dead, "and let's away, to part the glories of this happy day."

Then together they left the field . . .

Henry IV Part One

Though murdered kings, like all dead men, lie quiet and unoffending in the ground, they rot and spread contagion in men's minds. King Richard was in the earth, and nibbled clean by worms; but the kingdom festered with the consequences of his violent end.

In a sombre, cheerless chamber in the royal palace in London, the new King and his dukes and earls debated the troubled state of the land. There was war in Wales, there was war in Scotland, and there was war in the new King's heart. Bolingbroke – now King Henry the Fourth – longed to go to the Holy Land and fight for Christ, so that he might wash his soul free from the stain of murdered Richard's blood; but stern necessity compelled him to stay at home and fight for himself.

Guilt and kingship had aged him; those who had helped him to the throne, now resented him, and even good news was spiked with bad. Harry Percy, the Duke of Northumberland's brilliant son, known to all as Hotspur, had won a great victory in Scotland, which should have been cause for rejoicing – and would have been, had it not now seemed that the young man had been fighting more for himself than for his King. He had taken many rich Scottish prisoners, and would not give them up.

This impudent refusal, this bare-faced robbery of royal ransoms, greatly angered the King; but, at the same time, he could not help admiring the fierce young man's boldness and daring. Whatever Hotspur did, was done with courage and pride.

In his heart of hearts, King Henry envied the Duke of Northumberland and his glorious son. His own first-born, his own Harry, had turned out to be a hero only of the stews and taverns, and crown prince of riot and disorder.

"O that it could be proved," he sighed, "that some night-tripping fairy had exchanged in cradle-clothes our children where they lay . . . Then I would have his Harry and he mine . . ."

War and rebellion were heavy burdens on his shoulders, but his son's behaviour was an arrow in his heart. He shook his head and, with an effort, put aside his private distress. Hotspur, no matter how brightly he shone, had disobeyed him; and must answer for it.

While the King, with his dukes and earls, was thus engaged, considering matters of great moment, his son, Prince Hal, was likewise considering a matter of moment. Or, more particularly, the matter of *a* moment. In short, the time of day.

The Prince's apartment, in another part of the town, was somewhat more genial than his father's. In place of state papers were playbills and ballads; in place of serious earls were empty bottles; and in place of sober dukes was a portly knight, by name of Sir John Falstaff, asleep and snoring on a couch. His belt, huge enough to encompass a horse, was unbuckled, and his belly rose and fell like the sea.

For a moment, the Prince gazed down upon him, partly in humorous affection, and partly in wonderment, as if the day had wiped out all recollection of the night. They made a curious pair: the slender, handsome young Prince and the fat old man. They would seem to have had little in common but humanity – of which the sleeping knight, by reason of his enormous bulk, must have had the lion's share. The prince smiled; and, picking up a bottle, anointed the knight's bald head with some unaccountably forgotten drops of wine.

"Now, Hal," complained Falstaff, rising like a whale from his dreams, "what time of day is it, lad?"

"What a devil hast thou to do with the time of the day?" marvelled the Prince. "Unless hours were cups of sack," he went on, regarding the empty bottles and the blowsy, unbuttoned state of the knight, "and minutes capons, and clocks the tongues of bawds, and dials the signs of leaping-houses, and the blessed sun himself a fair hot wench in flame-coloured taffeta, I see no reason why thou should be so superfluous as to demand the time of the day."

"Indeed, you come near me now, Hal," admitted the fat old man, wiping the wine from his stained pate and delicately tasting his finger-ends, "for we that take purses go by the moon . . ."

So they fell to a cheerful bickering about stealing purses and repentance for such sins, with the young man making fun of his old companion – sometimes sharply enough to wound – and the knight affecting remorse and blaming the King's son for leading him astray.

"Thou hast done much harm upon me, Hal," he protested piously, "God forgive thee for it."

But in the very next moment, when the Prince slyly put the possibility before him, he was ready and eager to steal a purse wherever one might be had.

"From praying to purse-taking!" wondered the Prince, quite overcome by Falstaff's affable disregard for all law but his own.

"Why, Hal," explained Falstaff, quite unabashed, "'tis my vocation, Hal, 'tis no sin for a man to labour in his vocation!"

No sooner had he uttered this sentiment, in a high-pitched, churchly chant, and with an expression of fat religious devotion, than his best hopes were answered. Poins, a young friend of the Prince's, entered the apartment with an air of some excitement.

"Tomorrow morning," he announced, "by four o'clock early at Gad's Hill, there are pilgrims going to Canterbury with rich offerings, and traders riding to London with fat purses." It would be child's play – and it was play to such children – to waylay the travellers and rob them of all they had.

Falstaff beamed happily. He turned to the Prince.

"Hal, wilt thou make one?"

"Who, I rob?" returned the Prince indignantly. "I, a thief? Not I, by my faith!"

"There's neither honesty, manhood, nor good fellowship in thee," said Falstaff, disgusted by the unlooked-for honesty of his companion. But the Prince was unmoved; so Falstaff departed, leaving Poins to do what he could to change the Prince's mind.

No sooner had the fat knight flourished his bulk out of the room, than Poins laid his arm familiarly round the Prince's shoulders.

"Now my good, sweet honey lord," he murmured coaxingly, "ride with us tomorrow. I have a jest to execute that I cannot manage alone."

The jest was this: he and the Prince, together with Falstaff and his ruffianly associates, namely, Bardolph, Peto and Gadshill, should waylay the travellers; then Poins and the Prince should leave the others to rob them. "And when they have the booty," chuckled Poins, "if you and I do not rob them, cut this head from off my shoulders!"

The valour of Falstaff and his men being notorious, there was no doubt that Poins and the Prince would be more than a match for them.

"The virtue of this jest," Poins assured the Prince, "will be the incomprehensible lies that this same fat rogue will tell us when we meet at supper; of how thirty at least he fought with."

"Well, I'll go with thee," laughed the Prince. "Meet me tomorrow night in Eastcheap."

When Poins had gone, Prince Hal shrugged his shoulders, almost as if he wanted to shake off the memory of a too-familiar arm that had so lately rested upon them. He frowned. He both loved his companions, with their idle, lawless way, and despised them. Sooner or later, he knew, he would have to take on the heavy burden of kingship, and have done with Falstaff and his friends. And he would be the better for it. Yet, in his heart of hearts, he grieved. His present way of life was part of the folly of youth, which must be outgrown. Yet to outgrow the folly would be to outgrow youth. He sighed; and tried to comfort himself with the thought of how brightly he would shine when the time came for him to throw off his loose behaviour and stand before the world as the admired and glorious king.

While one Harry was idly dreaming of the glory that would be his, the other Harry was much concerned with the glory that *was* his. And he was going to keep it. Hotspur, the fiery son of the Duke of Northumberland, together with his father and his uncle, the Earl of Worcester, was at Windsor. He had come in answer to the King's summons and was prepared to defend his actions by attacking those of everybody else. They met in the council chamber where the King voiced his sharp displeasure, particularly against the Earl of Worcester, whom he blamed chiefly for Hotspur's defiance.

"Worcester, get thee gone," he commanded, "for I do see danger and disobedience in thine eye."

The Earl, thinly hiding his anger under a cloak of courtesy, withdrew. The King frowned after him; then, turning to Northumberland and his son, demanded to know why Hotspur had refused to deliver up his Scottish prisoners.

"My liege, I did deny no prisoners," responded Hotspur indignantly, forgetful of the fact that he had. It had been a misunderstanding, on account of the messenger the King had sent. Hotspur had not liked him. In fact, he was a person to whom Hotspur had taken the strongest exception. He had arrived on the battlefield at a bad time, when, as Hotspur put it, "I was dry with rage and extreme toil, breathless and faint, leaning upon my sword."

It seemed that the royal messenger had been one of those elegant gentlemen who had minced his way across the battlefield, and had complained faintly of the smell of corpses and the disagreeable nature of battlefields in general.

"He made me mad," exploded Hotspur at length, pacing the room in his agitation, now sitting, now standing, now confiding in the King's very ear, now addressing the ceiling, now the wall, "to see him shine so brisk and smell so sweet and talk so like a waiting-gentlewoman of guns and drums and wounds, God save the mark!"

In a word, Hotspur had lost his temper and had sent the King's messenger about his business without properly understanding what that business was.

The scene, as represented by the fierce young man, brought a smile even to the King's lips, and it was hard not to sympathise with him, for plainly he set valour and honour above everything; but he had done wrong. He had disobeyed his King and the conditions he had proposed for giving up his prisoners had only made matters worse. He had had the impudence to demand that his brother-in-law, Mortimer, who had been captured in Wales and was now held by the ferocious Owen Glendower, should be ransomed.

Now the King had no love for Mortimer, who had lately married Glendower's daughter and so become an ally of the enemy.

"I shall never hold that man my friend," pronounced the King, staring sombrely at Hotspur, "whose tongue shall ask me for one penny cost to ransom home revolted Mortimer."

"Revolted Mortimer!" shouted Hotspur, forgetful of respect in the royal presence. He was incensed by the unjust accusation and he rushed to his brother-in-law's defence. But the King would have nothing of it.

"Send us your prisoners," he said coldly, "or you will hear of it."

He and his attendant lords swept from the chamber, leaving Hotspur to burn with helpless rage. His father tried to calm him, but Hotspur's fire was not so easily put out. His uncle Worcester came quietly back into the chamber; and still Hotspur raged on about his brother-in-law, whose very name the King had forbidden him to pronounce.

As he raved, and strode, and banged the table, the father and the uncle exchanged interested looks. Surely all this wild energy could be put to a more profitable use? Imperceptibly they nodded; and the Earl of Worcester, almost by the way, remarked that the King could hardly be blamed for disliking Mortimer, for had not Mortimer been proclaimed, by dead King Richard, as his heir?

"He was," agreed Northumberland instantly, "I heard the proclamation."

Hotspur paused. He stared from his father to his uncle, and from his uncle to his father, as if scarcely able to believe what he had heard.

"But soft, I pray you," he demanded, breathing deeply, "did King Richard then proclaim my brother Edmund Mortimer heir to the crown?"

"He did," confirmed Northumberland, "myself did hear it."

Then he and Worcester, the two seasoned men of power, stood back, as it were, to warm their dangerous hearts and dangerous hands at Hotspur's wild blaze. They hated the King and sought only to uncrown him. But to do it, they needed Hotspur. They would be the shaft of rebellion's spear, but he, admired by all for his high honour, must be the brightly shining tip. They knew that Hotspur would not stir unless honour was at stake, so they had given him cause to join with them against the thankless, dishonourable King.

Patiently they waited for him to have done raging against, "this thorn, this canker, Bolingbroke . . . this vile politician, Bolingbroke," then they put it to him that there were others of a like mind. Eagerly the young man listened; and then and there, in the King's own council chamber, the rebellion against the throne began.

While the Harry of the north was thus preparing for his great enterprise, which was to be no less than hurling a dishonourable king from a doubtful throne, in other words, robbing a robber, Harry of the south was already out and about upon a similar enterprise . . . although on a more modest scale.

Four o'clock of a black morning on the highway at Gad's Hill. Fearful hissings and creepings in the bushy dark, and a huge lurking robber quaking with anger.

"A plague upon it when thieves cannot be true one to another!" cursed Falstaff, abandoned by his companions and left alone.

There came a faint whistling from the darkness, as of soused and bleary nightingales. "A plague upon you all," raged Falstaff, brandishing his sword to the terror of the bushes, "give me my horse, you rogues, give me my horse and be hanged!"

"Peace, ye fat guts," whispered Prince Hal, creeping out of the shadows, "lie down, lay thine ear close to the ground and list if thou canst hear the tread of travellers."

"Have you any levers to lift me up again," demanded the fat knight, "being down? I prithee, good Prince Hal, help me to my horse, good King's son."

Indignantly the Prince declined.

"Hang thyself in thine own heir-apparent garters!" snarled Falstaff, and threatened that, if he should be taken, he would inform on his friends without hesitation.

Shadows stirred, grass rustled and twigs snapped. Each from his hole of darkness, the robbers appeared. They whispered together. Falstaff and his men – four in all, and armed to the blackened teeth with pistols, cudgels, swords, daggers and determination – were to lie in wait for the travellers in the narrow lane. Poins and the Prince were to hide further down the hill, so that any who escaped the first ambush would be caught by the second. Much nodding and grinning and glinting of eyes . . . Be quiet! Travellers were coming! How many? Some eight or ten . . .

"Zounds, will they not rob us?" wondered Falstaff uneasily.

The travellers drew near, toiling wearily up the hill. Hastily Poins and the Prince vanished into the night.

"Now, my masters," breathed Falstaff, valiantly grasping his sword, which seemed no bigger than a tooth-pick beside his vast bulk, "every man to his business."

The travellers appeared, no more than four round-faced innocents, jingling with purses and property.

"Stand!" bellowed the thieves.

"Jesus bless us!" shrieked the merchants; and there followed a fearful scene of curses, thumps and grunts as the ravening wolves fell upon the hapless lambs

142

and robbed them of all they possessed. It was over in moments, and the thieves made off, leaving the merchants trussed up in a bundle of shaking legs and rolling eyes.

Poins and the Prince came out of concealment, nodded to one another, and silently followed Falstaff and his men. Presently they came upon them as they were about to share out their gains. The young men, cloaked and hooded, hid behind trees, and listened.

". . . and the Prince and Poins be not two arrant cowards," grunted Falstaff, who had seen nothing of the young men during the desperate duel with the merchants. "There's no equity stirring; there's no more valour in that Poins than in a wild duck."

The young men drew their swords.

"Your money!" roared the Prince, in a voice of thunder.

"Villains!" bellowed Poins in a voice as terrible; and the pair of them rushed out upon the startled four.

The bold thieves turned faces white as milk; and then, without pausing to reckon the odds, abandoned their profit and fled. Falstaff alone stayed to make one or two valiant flourishes with his sword; but then, valuing his life above his livelihood, he too departed, whisking through the night like a runaway bull, bellowing with rage and terror.

The two young men gathered up the purses that had been left behind. They were almost helpless with laughter at the ease with which they had robbed the robbers.

Conspiring lords, no less than thieves, fall out; and there's betrayal and abandoning of friends in the higher world of politics no less than in the lower one of highway robbery. Hotspur had received a letter in his castle at Warkworth. It was from a gentleman on

143

whom he'd counted for assistance, and who was now crying off.

"The purpose you undertake is dangerous," he read. He looked up. He scowled. "Why, that's certain," he muttered contemptuously. "'Tis dangerous to take a cold, to sleep, to drink; but I tell you, my lord fool, out of this nettle, danger, we pluck this flower, safety." He continued with the letter, becoming more and more exasperated with the writer's objections to the great enterprise. At length he flung the letter aside.

"By the Lord!" he exploded. "Our plot is a good plot, as ever was laid, our friends true and constant and full of expectation; an excellent plot, very good friends. Zounds, and I were now by this rascal," (he kicked angrily at the crumpled letter), "I could brain him with his lady's fan. Is there not my father, my uncle and myself?" he demanded, listing his fellow conspirators upon his fingers, "Lord Edmund Mortimer, my lord of York and Owen Glendower? Is there not, besides, the Douglas? Have I not all their letters to meet me in arms by the ninth of the next month?"

Then, after some further unflattering remarks about the letter writer, he decided he would set out that very night to meet with his dangerous friends. He told his pretty wife that he must go, but not why, or where.

"What is it carries you away?" she demanded.

"Why, my horse, my love, my horse," said he.

"Out, you mad-headed ape!" she cried. "I'll know your business, Harry, that I will."

But plead, threaten and cajole as she might, he would not tell her; and only in the moment of parting did he relent sufficiently to promise:

"Whither I go, thither shall you go too; today will I set forth, tomorrow you."

In the Boar's Head Tavern – a frowsy hostelry with as many nooks and cubbyholes as a nibbled cheese – the

Harry of the south thought briefly of his glorious counterpart, that world's idol and pattern of honour. He shrugged his shoulders ruefully.

"I am not yet of Percy's mind," he confided to Poins, as the pair of them awaited the return of Falstaff from Gad's Hill, "the Hotspur of the north, he that kills me some six or seven dozen of Scots at a breakfast, washes his hands and says to his wife, 'Fie upon this quiet life, I want work . . .'"

Poins laughed; and so did Prince Hal, but with a touch of bitterness, as if he partly envied what he mocked. Then all thoughts of honour and glory were blown to the winds as, with a clatter of boots and a commotion of oaths, Falstaff and his men arrived. Torn, muddy and sweating from their adventure, they collapsed upon benches and chairs. Falstaff looked hard at Poins and the Prince.

"A plague of all cowards, I say," he remarked sombrely. "Give me a cup of sack, boy." A cup was fetched. He drank and made a sour face. He glared at the potboy. "You rogue, here's lime in this sack . . . yet a coward is worse than a cup of sack with lime in it."

To prove it, he turned his fat back on Poins and the Prince and drank again. Addressing his companions, and studiously ignoring the Prince, he continued to abuse cowards; until the Prince ventured to inquire the cause of his displeasure. Falstaff turned.

"Are you not a coward?" he demanded. "Answer me to that – and Poins there?"

"Zounds, ye fat paunch," cried Poins angrily, "and ye call me a coward, by the Lord, I'll stab thee!"

"I call thee coward?" wondered Falstaff, putting a table between himself and the indignant Poins. "I'll see thee damned 'ere I call thee coward, but I would give a thousand pound I could run as fast as thou canst."

At last the reason for the knight's black mood came

out. The adventure upon Gad's Hill. In spite of monumental heroism, the like of which the world had never seen, it had been a defeat. He and his three fearless companions (who dimly nodded their battered heads) had boldly robbed some sixteen ferocious merchants; and then had had the cruel misfortune to be set upon and robbed themselves. (Again the companions nodded.) By how many? the Prince inquired, with a sly glance at Poins. By a hundred, at least, said Falstaff unblushingly; and even his companions gaped at the enormity of the lie.

"What, a hundred, man?" cried the Prince.

"I am a rogue if I were not at half-sword with a dozen of them two hours together," said Falstaff modestly, and went on to describe so desperate a battle that even a Hotspur would have paled at. Enemies, which seemed to multiply, as if they'd been put out at compound interest, came at him from every corner of the night; but still he duelled and still he fought, holding them all at bay – until, most treacherously, he was overcome.

"Three misbegotten knaves in Kendal green came at my back," he said bitterly, "and let drive at me, for it was so dark, Hal, that thou couldst not see thy hand."

The Prince nodded. Falstaff sighed and drank again, to drown the memory of that frightful time. Then the Prince called him a fat liar. Falstaff, much offended, demanded to know why. The Prince told him. How could he have known that the misbegotten knaves were in Kendal green when it was so dark he could not see his hand? Loftily, Falstaff declined to answer; so the Prince, with grim pleasure, went on to demolish the fat old man by telling him that the hundred he'd fought against had been no more than two; himself and Poins.

"What trick, what device, what starting-hole canst

thou now find out," demanded the Prince, "to hide thee from this open and apparent shame?"

Falstaff was silent. His little eyes, like mice in a mansion, peeped from side to side. He frowned. He gnawed his lip. Then he beamed.

"By the Lord," he exclaimed, slapping his mighty knee with his plump hand, "I knew thee as well as he that made thee! Why, hear you, my masters," he asked of the company, "was it for me to kill the heir-apparent? Could I turn upon the true Prince?"

With huge innocence he turned from face to face, and outfaced them all. There was no demolishing Falstaff. The truth rebounded from his fat person as harmlessly as a spent arrow, and to accuse him of lying was like blaming the ocean for being wet. There was nothing for it but to laugh . . . at truth and lies and life itself.

In the midst of all the merriment, there came, like a spectre to the feast, a gentleman from the court with a message for the Prince from the King, his father. Falstaff went to inquire, and came back with uneasy news. Hotspur, Northumberland and Worcester, together with many powerful friends, were up in arms. The rebellion had begun.

"Thy father's beard," said the fat man, "is turned white with the news; you may buy land now as cheap as stinking mackerel."

The Prince was commanded to appear before his father in the morning; for, when all was said and done, Hal was the heir-apparent, and, when all was said and done, the King had need of him. Earnestly Falstaff exhorted his young friend to prepare himself and have some ready answer to the heavy reproaches that the King would undoubtedly heap upon his son's way of life. The Prince looked at the old man thoughtfully. Suddenly he laughed.

"Do thou stand for my father and examine me upon the particulars of my life."

Falstaff blinked. A look of startled fondness flickered across his wine-red face. "Shall I?" he wondered. He beamed. "Content!" he cried; and, settling himself royally in his chair, crowned his bald pate with a dirty tasselled cushion. Then, to the huge delight of the assembled thieves, potboys, and the blotchy hostess of the tavern, who was weeping and hiccuping with laughter, he addressed the Prince with all the dignity of a sorrowing father and a troubled king.

Meekly, and with bowed head, the Prince listened as his father, in the person of the raddled old knight, reproached him for his wild ways and low companions.

"And yet there is a virtuous man whom I have often noted in thy company," said Falstaff dreamily.

"What manner of man, and it like Your Majesty?" inquired the Prince, as if he did not know.

"A good portly man, i'faith," said Falstaff happily, "and a corpulent, of a cheerful look, a pleasing eye, and a most noble carriage; and now I remember me, his name is Falstaff . . ." He paused for the roars of laughter to die down, and then said most sincerely: "There is virtue in that Falstaff; him keep with, the rest banish . . ."

"Dost thou speak like a king?" interrupted the Prince, smiling, but with an edge to his voice; for Falstaff's open mockery of his father and himself had affected him more deeply than might have been supposed. "Do thou stand for me, and I'll play my father."

Cheerfully, and with a better grace than King Richard (whom Hal's father had deposed) the fat man resigned his throne and crown. He stood, humbly, before the new king, biting his thumbnail and tracing a pattern with his toe, the very image of an awkward prince. The Prince himself, seated in the chair of state, and wearing the cushion, regarded his mockery self with elaborate severity. The company laughed, expecting more comedy; and so indeed it began, with stern questions from the son-father and meek, apologetic answers from the father-son ... for Falstaff had years enough to be Hal's father, and even his grandfather as well. Then the mood changed. The young man's voice grew harder, and his very youth seemed turned to stone.

"There is a devil haunts thee," he said, as if looking through Falstaff to himself, "in the likeness of an old fat man, a tun of man is thy companion. Why dost thou converse with that trunk of humours, that bolting-hutch of beastliness, that swollen parcel of dropsies ... that reverend vice, that grey iniquity, that father ruffian ..."

Mercilessly the Prince went on. Laughter died, smiles faded, and Falstaff himself grew uneasy, not because of the brutality of the young man's words, but because of what he dreaded might be in the young man's heart. This was the fat knight's only weakness: his deep love for Hal. It was the only point in his armour of lying, boastfulness and dishonesty through which he could be hurt.

"If to be old and merry," he protested, anxiously trying to defend himself, "be a sin, then many an old host that I know is damned ... banish Peto, banish Bardolph, banish Poins – but for sweet Jack Falstaff ... banish not him thy Harry's company ... banish plump Jack, and banish all the world."

"I do, I will," said the Prince coldy; and at that moment he was indeed his father, the lean stern politician, Bolingbroke.

Urgently Falstaff attempted to plead more on his own behalf, when there came a loud knocking on the tavern door. The sheriff and the watch had come in search of the robbers from Gad's Hill. In particular, they were looking for a gross fat man ...

149

Instantly Falstaff hid; and the Prince, forgetting everything but fondness, lied to save his friend.

"The man I do assure you," he promised the sheriff, "is not here."

Not satisfied, but forced to take the Prince's word, the sheriff departed. Falstaff was looked for and discovered fast asleep behind a curtain. He was quite worn out from all his labours and all his frights. Upon a sudden impulse, the Prince told Peto search the snorer's pockets. Nothing was found but a list of debts. The Prince sighed. All Falstaff's substance was in his flesh; he owned nothing but the listed recollections of food and drink. Hal shrugged his shoulders and departed to meet with his father, leaving behind the lying, boastful, laughing world of Falstaff for the grim world of honour, politics and war.

Of all the discontented barons who had gathered under the banner of Hotspur and Northumberland, none was more feared than Owen Glendower. Even Falstaff had quaked at the mention of him, for he was said to have power over the spirits and demons of the air. Deep in his Welsh stronghold, he strode back and forth, a short, fierce gentleman in a robe of silver stars and moons that billowed out behind him, and with a nose like the prow of a ship and deep-set eyes that burned like hot cannons. In rolling Welsh tones, he informed his companions – Hotspur, Mortimer and Worcester – that he was so remarkable a personage that, at his birth, there had been strange portents in the sky and that the world itself had shaken.

Hotspur yawned. He had had more than his fill of wild Welsh magic. "Why so it would have done at the same season," he said, "if your mother's cat had but kitten'd, though yourself had never been born."

"I say the earth did shake when I was born,"

repeated Glendower, glaring at the impudent young man.

Hotspur said it did not; and the others, fearing for Glendower's rage, tried to keep Hotspur quiet. It was a hopeless task.

"I can call spirits from the vasty deep," said Glendower, darkly.

"Why, so can I," said Hotspur, not much impressed, "or so can any man, but will they come when you do call for them?"

It was an uncomfortable beginning to the enterprise; but then Hotspur was an uncomfortable young man. He lacked an easy temper. Unlike the other Harry, he could never have lived and laughed with a Falstaff. He loved honour too much, and he suspected all the world of trying to rob him of it. Presently, however, the differences between Hotspur and Glendower were resolved and the meeting ended with the coming in of wives, and Lady Mortimer singing a sweet song in Welsh and Lady Percy making amorous fun of her husband, so that, for a little while, honour, politics and war gave way to music, smiles and love.

Prince Hal stood before the King. He tried with all his might to look serious and contrite; but as his lean, stern father talked and frowned and sadly shook his head, and reproached him for his wild ways and low companions, the young man could not help thinking that his father was very like a thin imitation of Falstaff imitating the King. Then his father spoke, as he always did, of Hotspur, the too-glorious Hotspur. Even though Hotspur had rebelled against him, he was still admired; and, Hal knew, preferred above himself.

"What never-dying honour he hath got," went on the King, driving knives of envy into his son's heart, "against renowned Douglas . . ."

Silently the Prince stood as his father continued to heap praises upon the bright Harry of the north, at the expense of the dull Harry who stood before him. "Thou art degenerate," accused the King.

"Do not think so," cried Hal, "you shall not find it so!" and he poured out his bitterness against Hotspur and swore that he would prove himself to be the better man. "For the time will come," he promised, "that I shall make this northern youth exchange his glorious deeds for my indignities!"

So fiercely did he speak that the King's heart quickened and, for the first time, he saw in his son some glimmerings of the greatness he had hoped for; and when news came in that the rebels were gathering at Shrewsbury, he gladly gave the Prince command over an army to march against them.

"Let's away," he urged, laying a fond arm about his son's shoulders. "Advantage feeds him fat while men delay."

"Bardolph, am I not fallen away?" sighed Falstaff to his purple-nosed companion as the pair of them slopped into the Boar's Head Tavern. "Do I not bate? Do I not dwindle?" he wondered, patting his huge belly and finding it to be some inches from where he expected it. He sat down and regarded his countenance in the diminishing bowl of a spoon. "Why, my skin hangs about me like an old lady's loose-gown."

He was melancholy. It was not so much Falstaff as the world that was falling away. War was approaching, and his beloved Hal was now with his true father. The fat man felt himself neglected. He turned quarrelsome and accused the hostess of picking his pocket while he'd slept.

"I have lost," he complained bitterly, "a seal-ring of my grandfather's worth forty mark."

"O Jesu," cried the hostess indignantly, "I have

heard the Prince tell him, I know not how oft, that that ring was copper!"

"The Prince is a Jack, a sneak-up!" snarled Falstaff, venting his spleen on the absent young man, "'sblood, and were he here I would cudgel him like a dog."

Even as he uttered the threat, the Prince came marching in. He was fresh and spruce and shining from his father's presence, and every inch the heir-apparent to the throne. At once the knight's melancholy left him; and he glowed as if his Hal had kindled him.

"Now, Hal, to the news at court," he demanded eagerly. "For the robbery, lad, how is that answered?"

All was well. The money had been paid back and Falstaff was no longer in danger from the sheriff. The Prince was good friends with his father; and, what was more, had procured Falstaff the command of a company of soldiers. The Prince was in high good spirits. The prospect of battle excited him, and the thought of meeting, at last, with his great rival, filled him with a fierce eagerness.

"The land is burning," he cried, "Percy stands on high, and either we or they must lower lie!"

"Rare words!" chuckled Falstaff, when the warlike Prince had gone. "Brave world!" And he settled down to eat his breakfast with an appetite restored.

Messengers crossed and re-crossed the land, galloping down narrow lanes and along broad highways on steaming horses, carrying rumour in their looks and news in their saddle-bags, from north to south, from south to north, to the King in London and to the rebel lords in Shrewsbury as the country plunged and staggered towards war. News came to Hotspur as he waited with Douglas and Worcester for his father and Glendower to join them, that his father was sick in bed and could not come. This was a great blow and

153

Worcester cast doubts upon the sickness which he suspected to be caused more by caution than infection. Scarcely had this disaster been taken in than more messengers came, like doom-croaking ravens, to the rebel camp. Owen Glendower was delayed, and the King with all his people, was up in arms and marching north.

"What may the King's whole battle reach unto?" demanded Hotspur.

"To thirty thousand," answered the messenger.

"Forty let it be!" cried Hotspur, not in the least dismayed; for this was the cream of honour, to battle against impossible odds.

But the odds were not quite so great as Hotspur had been told. Already, and without a shot being fired or a sword being raised, the King's great army had been reduced by a hundred and fifty. How so? Falstaff had sold them. By the authority entrusted to him, he had pressed into service only those who were rich enough to buy themselves out; in their place the knight was now the captain of some three hundred pounds and a band of ragged skeletons who had scarcely strength enough to march. Quilted, plumed and tasselled, like a pavilion filled with a gust of wind, the fat warrior rolled along the road to Coventry while his miserable little army picked their way painfully in his wake. Prince Hal, riding with the Lord of Westmoreland, came upon him and urged him to make haste, for the King's forces were already at Shrewsbury. He glanced back, and saw Falstaff's regiment.

"Tell me, Jack," he asked, "whose fellows are these that come after?"

"Mine, Hal, mine," responded Falstaff proudly.

"I did never see such pitiful rascals!"

"Tut, tut," exclaimed Falstaff, loftily waving aside all criticism, "good enough to toss, food for powder,

154

food for powder . . ." he chuckled, "they'll fill a pit as well as better; tush, man, mortal men, mortal men."

The Prince frowned. Falstaff's harsh humour was not to his present taste.

"Sirrah, make haste!" he commanded. "Percy is already in the field!"

It was night-time in the rebel camp, and lanterns peered among the tents like creeping glow-worms. Hotspur was impatient for the coming battle. Time and again Douglas and Worcester urged him to wait until more men came in to swell his force. But Hotspur was a hero in the old style: caution, to him, was little better than cowardice.

A trumpet sounded, thin as a knife in the night. Voices murmured, lanterns gathered and threw up in their combined light, a herald emblazoned with the gaudy lions of the King. It was Sir Walter Blunt, a much-respected gentleman, come with an offer from the King. Swiftly he was conducted to Hotspur, who greeted him with affection and listened to him with courtesy. The message was that the King would know what were Hotspur's grievances so that they might be remedied without loss of blood. It was, all things considered, a fair and generous offer. But not to Hotspur, who admired the messenger but not the sender of the message.

"The King is kind," he said bitterly, "and well we know the King knows at what time to promise, when to pay," and then went on to deliver so damning an account of the King's misdeeds and the King's ingratitude, that no king could have endured it and remained a king.

"Shall I return this answer to the King?" asked Sir Walter, whose patience had been strained by the young man's furious recital of the wrongs done him.

Hotspur paused, and shook his head. The reproach

in the herald's voice had moved him. "Not so, Sir Walter," he replied at length. "We'll withdraw awhile . . . go to the King . . . and in the morning early shall mine uncle bring him our purposes . . ."

"I would you would accept of grace and love," urged Sir Walter.

"And may be so we shall," returned Hotspur, but more out of kindness than belief.

The morning was pale and the sun bloody. It glinted on helmets and breast-plates like painted wounds. A herald's approach was sounded, and Worcester, that discontented, dangerous Earl, presented himself before the King. He had brought Hotspur's answer. It was violent and intemperate. Tight-lipped, he listened to the accusations of ingratitude, double-dealing and dishonourable theft of the crown. In part, he knew them to be true; but he was the King, and that high office absolved him from the crimes of private men. He was answerable only to God and his own heart. Government was all. Coldly he dismissed the accusations as being no more than the gilding of insurrection.

Prince Hal, stern in unaccustomed steel, stood beside his father. He surveyed the ranked soldiers whose pale faces looked anxiously at the day, as if wondering if they should see another.

"In both your armies," he said to the scowling Earl, "there is many a soul shall pay full dearly for this encounter if once they join in trial." He made no attempt to rebut Hotspur's charges or even to defend his father's name; instead, after paying due homage to Hotspur's courage and high honour, he offered himself in single combat against the other Harry, so that the blood of many might be saved.

It was a brave and chivalrous speech; it was a young man's speech; it was also, in the King's opinion, a

156

foolish speech. It harked back to the old days of tournaments, that were long out of fashion.

"And, Prince of Wales, so dare we venture thee," he said, in public recognition of his son's valour; but then went on in a shrewder vein: "Albeit, considerations infinite do make against it."

This king was not so foolish as to risk all on one man's courage, particularly when he himself had the advantage in numbers. Besides, he suspected that his own Harry would be no match for the other. Accordingly he dismissed Worcester with no more than the offer of a pardon if the rebels would lay down their arms. Otherwise, they must take the dreadful consequences.

"We offer fair," he said. "Take it advisedly."

"It will not be accepted," said the Prince, when Worcester had departed. "The Douglas and the Hotspur both together are confident against the world in arms."

The King nodded. He knew that the battle must come.

"God befriend us," he said, as if to reassure his son, "as our cause is just."

He moved away, and with him went all the assembled earls, lords and captains, clanking grimly in their steel. The Prince, momentarily alone, frowned as he thought of the coming fight, of proud Hotspur who risked everything for honour, and of his father who risked nothing; of the justice of Hotspur's accusations, and the deviousness of his father's ways ... and of good men dying for another's cause.

A loud clatter broke in on his thoughts, a mighty clashing, as of a kitchen in a gale. It was Falstaff in armour, and overflowing it, like too large a feast crammed into too few pots and pans. His breastplate lay upon his chest like a small tureen.

"Hal," he said uneasily, "if thou see me down in the battle and bestride me, so. 'Tis a point of friendship."

The Prince smiled ruefully at the fat and fearful old man. "Say thy prayers, and farewell."

"I would 'twere bed-time, Hal, and all well."

"Why, thou owest God a death," said the Prince.

"'Tis not due yet," cried Falstaff indignantly; but the Prince had gone to make ready for the battle. Falstaff shrugged his shoulders, and his armour chimed like church bells. He stared round at the little world of fluttering banners and painted shields, of kings and princes, and shivering wretches preparing to kill each other ... for no better reason than for honour. He frowned, as if mightily puzzled.

"Can honour set to a leg?" he wondered. He pondered deeply; then shook his head. "No. Or an arm? No. Or take away the grief of a wound? No. Honour hath no skill in surgery then? No." He looked mournful, as if it was a real sorrow to him that honour could not undo the harm that honour had done. "What is honour?" he demanded. He thought again. "A word. Who hath it? Him that died a-Wednesday. Doth he feel it? No. Doth he hear it? No." With each repetition of the word honour, it seemed to become more meaningless. "I'll none of it!" grunted Falstaff at length; and, with a further shrug of his fat, plated shoulders, went off to lead his gnawed lambs to the slaughter.

Worcester returned to the rebel camp. He said nothing of the offered pardon. He knew, full well, that it would never be extended to him. He would be made to bear the blame for all. His only hope lay in the chance of battle, and he was prepared to shed the blood of thousands to save his own. No matter; Hotspur's bright glory would cover all; for many misshapen creatures creep along under the richly embroidered cloak of honour.

The sky was melancholy; and the wind, blustering across the field outside Shrewsbury, seemed to cause the opposing forces to bend and tremble, like the shaking of wheat. Suddenly tiny voices shouted; trumpets shrieked as if in fright; and the ground began to shudder under the advancing thunder of horses' hooves. Slowly at first, and then with gathering speed, the armies rushed towards each other, so that, for a moment, they might have been intent upon a wild and joyous meeting. Then they met.

Shouts and screams of men and horses filled the air. Cannons roared; bright figures crashed and struggled; thick flowers of dust bloomed among them, and spreading, formed a huge rolling cloud that obscured all but the jagged edges of the conflict. Within this hellish cloud, men ran hither and thither, bleeding, screaming, cursing, looking for other men to kill. Among them, Hotspur searched for the other Harry, and the other Harry searched for him. Fat Falstaff searched for safety; and the wild Scot, Douglas, searched to kill the King. But the world, that day, seemed full of kings; that careful man, the true King, had dressed many in his armour. See! here was another! Douglas attacked, and in moments the royal armour fell and blood rushed out of it. Hotspur appeared, like the spirit of battle.

"All's done, all's won!" panted Douglas, "here breathless lies the King!"

But it was only another image he had killed; it was Sir Walter Blunt.

"Up and away!" cried Hotspur; and the two great soldiers vanished into the murky air.

There was quiet for a moment; and safety. The large shape of Falstaff appeared, very cautiously, as if he was squeezing sideways through a narrow gap in the air. He advanced, clutching a sword that had seen much action, but had wisely taken no part in it. He stumbled over the dead man.

"Soft! Who are you? Sir Walter Blunt – there's honour for you!"

He shook his head; then looked about him as if for his followers. There were none. He shrugged his shoulders, and sighed:

"I have led my ragamuffins where they are peppered; there's not three of my hundred and fifty left alive, and they are for the town's end to beg during life."

Hal found him.

"What, standst thou idle here?" he demanded angrily. "Lend me thy sword."

But Falstaff would not part with it. Instead he offered his pistol.

"Give it me; what, is it in the case?"

"Ay, Hal," apologised Falstaff, "'tis hot, 'tis hot . . ."

The Prince took the case and drew out, not a pistol, but a bottle of sack. Furiously the Prince threw it at the fat man who mocked everything, and rushed away in search of Hotspur, his heart's enemy. Ruefully Falstaff stared after the enraged Prince; then he glanced down at the dead man. He shuddered.

"I like not such grinning honour as Sir Walter hath. Give me life," he grunted; and crept away, glinting and clanking, to find some safer place.

The smoky air seemed full of holes, like clearings in a noisy roaring forest, beyond which could be seen the shadowy shapes of struggling men. In one such clearing stood the King, the true King. His companions had left him to stiffen resistance where it faltered, so that briefly he was alone. An armoured figure came out of the dust. It was Douglas!

"Another king!" he shouted. "They grow like Hydra's heads . . . What art thou that counterfeit'st the person of a king?"

"The King himself."

160

"I fear thou art another counterfeit!" cried Douglas; but nevertheless, attacked.

The Scot was the younger man, and the stronger, and the true King staggered under his blows. In moments he would have fallen and joined all his images in death, so that true and false would have been one; but the Prince appeared. At once he drew off Douglas, and they fought. Douglas was fierce and powerful, but Hal had learned his fighting, not on the field of chivalry, but in the murky lanes and byways where cut-throats lurked. He was more than a match for Douglas who, cursing, fled.

Hal extended his hand to his fallen father and drew him upright. The two looked deeply at one another; and, for a moment, in the smoke, fury and shrieks of the battle, there was a moment of reconciliation and peace. Then the King left the Prince and, even as he did so, the terrible moment came towards which Prince Hal's life had always been moving. Hotspur found him.

The two Harrys stared at one another almost with curiosity: the one who had just saved his father, and the other whose father had abandoned him in his need.

"Two stars," said Hal grimly, "keep not their motion in one sphere, nor can one England brook a double reign of Harry Percy and the Prince of Wales."

"Nor shall it, Harry," returned Hotspur, "for the hour is come to end the one of us."

So at last they fought, as it was certain that they should from the very beginning; and it seemed that all the world hung upon the outcome of the single combat that Hal had first proposed, and that his cautious father had rejected. But the real cause for which they struck and stabbed and hacked at each other, for which they glared and bled and hopped like iron toads, was not for the fate of kingdoms; nor was it for honour, but for the jealousy of honour.

Unknowingly they had attracted an onlooker. It was as if the brightness of the conflict had drawn a bloated moth. Falstaff hovered, anxiously watching the progress of the fight.

"To it, Hal!" he urged his beloved Prince. "Nay, you shall find no boy's play here, I can tell you!"

So intent was he on watching the conflict, that, before he knew it, he himself was set upon by Douglas, still searching for kings. He was too heavy to run, and too fat to dodge, so he exchanged one or two valiant blows with the fierce Scot, and, as soon as he conveniently could, fell to earth with a dreadful clatter and a dying grunt. And then lay still. Douglas left him; and, at that very instant, Hal stabbed Hotspur to the heart.

"O Harry, thou hast robbed me of my youth!" sighed Hotspur, as he lay, and bitterly whispered away the last of his life. "Percy," he breathed, "thou art dust, and food for – "

"For worms, brave Percy," completed the Prince; for Hotspur was dead. Sadly now the conquering Harry looked down on his rival; and grieved. He knew that he had killed not only Hotspur's youth but his own.

Suddenly he spied the huge form of Falstaff, lying like a fallen world; and his grief passed from the general to the sharply particular.

"What, old acquaintance," he wept, "could not all this flesh keep in a little life? Poor Jack, farewell! I could have better spared a better man."

He left the scene of the dead hero and the coward; and, so much for the dues of honour, his tears were for the coward.

An eye opened in Falstaff's head. It swivelled cautiously from side to side. Safety. Falstaff arose. "The better part of valour," said the knight, "is discretion, in the which better part I have saved my life."

His wandering gaze fell upon the dead Hotspur.

Alarm seized him. What if he was not quite dead? "Why may not he rise as well as I?" wondered Falstaff fearfully. He looked carefully about him. Nervously he raised his sword. "Nobody sees me," he muttered; and, with a quick movement, stabbed the dead man through the thigh.

Hotspur made no defence. "Come you along with me," grunted Falstaff; and began to heave the remains of the hero on to his broad back.

While he was thus engaged, the Prince and his younger brother returned to the scene. They stared at the resurrected Falstaff in amazement. The knight, quite unabashed at having been caught out in so gross a deception, regarded the two Princes with fat pride. He cast down Hotspur's misused body, declaring:

"There is Percy. If your father will do me any honour, so: if not, let him kill the next Percy himself. I look to be either earl or duke, I can assure you."

The Prince's wonderment turned to indignation.

"Why, Percy I killed myself, and saw thee dead."

"Didst thou?" said Falstaff pityingly. "Lord, Lord, how this world is given to lying! I grant you I was down, and out of breath, and so was he, but we rose both at an instant and fought a long hour by Shrewsbury clock."

Prince Hal, much divided between the claims of pride, honour, and old friendship, shook his head and smiled.

"If a lie may do thee grace," he murmured to the old rogue who, in many ways, had been a wiser and a better father to him than his own, "I'll gild it with the happiest terms I have."

A trumpet sounded, the rebels were in retreat. The King had won the day; and Hotspur, with all his honour, justice and high nobility, was in the dust. But Falstaff had survived.

"I'll follow," he said, preparing to roll on after the

victors, "as they say, for reward. He that rewards me, God reward him."

So the fat man strode on, with his head high and his chest thrust out, but some little way behind his paunch.

More work was to be done. Battles were to be won against Mortimer, Glendower and the Duke of Northumberland. But the King was confident. The father had forgiven his son; all that now remained was for the son to forgive his father.

The Taming of the Shrew

In the county of Warwickshire there lived a tinker, who, in his time, had followed many trades, and caught up with none. He was Christopher Sly by name, and coarse, drunken and brutish by nature.

"You will not pay for the glasses you have burst?" demanded the hostess of the inn he patronised.

For answer, he shook his fat head, belched, and lay down on the floor. The hostess, a female as sweet as a lemon, threatened him with a constable.

"Let him come," mumbled Sly, and, endeavouring to pull a stool over him as if it was a blanket, fell like a corpse into a tomb of snores. The hostess shook her fist and departed.

But before she could return, a most extraordinary thing happened to Christopher Sly. There was a sound of horns (which he heard not) and a barking of dogs. Then, flushed from galloping the countryside, a plumed and booted lord accompanied by huntsmen and servants, strode into the inn. They looked about them and saw, under a table, the drunken tinker, his pig-like countenance wreathed in smiles of ale. The lord shuddered, "Grim death, how foul and loathsome is thine image!" he exclaimed, somewhat fancifully although it must be admitted that Christopher Sly might as well have been dead for all he knew of lords and huntsmen and the world about him.

Then the lord, whose head was well-stocked with old tales of gods changing humans into swine, thought it an excellent idea to change this swinish tinker into a lord. Accordingly he told his servants to carry the snoring Sly to his mansion, wash him, improve him with perfumes, lay him in the richest chamber, and, when he woke, to bow to him, call him 'lord', offer him the best of food and drink and clothing, show him a simpering, girlish page-boy dressed up as his lady wife, and to explain to him that he had just awakened from a long lunacy during which he had only imagined that he was a tinker called Christopher Sly. Then, to fuddle him further, he was to be shown a play, and it was to be performed so straight and serious that he would no longer know what was true and what was make-believe. Then the lord went off, like one of the gods of old, to watch the transformation of the tinker into something rich and strange.

Christopher Sly woke up. He blinked, through eyes like stained-glass windows. He was in a room as gorgeous as a palace and was sitting on a mountain of cushions; and there were servants bowing all round him. He was not surprised. The world often looked queer when he woke up but after he'd had a drink or two, it turned ordinary again. "For God's sake, a pot of small ale!" he cried urgently. This time the vision did not fade; instead it grew more visionary and unreal. He was offered all manner of delicate things, quite unsuited to a tinker's tastes; and, when he objected, he was told that there was no such person as Christopher Sly, that Christopher Sly had only been a long bad dream, and that he was really a lord who had only just awakened from it.

He blinked again and thumped his head. Then music began to twink and scrape and a smiling gentleman talked of Apollos and Daphnes and suchlike, which was all Greek to Sly; and then a female appeared, pretty as a page-boy with a bosom as neat as a pair of oranges, and, most wonderful, she was his lady wife! This was plain good English to the tinker, who straightway wanted to take her to bed. But alas! this was not to be. He had been sick for so long, that he must husband his husband-strength awhile, lest his malady return. He and his lady-wife were to sit modestly side by side and watch a play. A play? He had never seen a play in his life before and did not know in the least what to expect; but he was ready to put up with anything rather than risk falling back into the horrible dream of being Christopher Sly.

Of a sudden, there was a loud flourish on a trumpet, that made the tinker jump; and the chamber grew as quiet as an empty church. Then, before the tinker's very eyes, the strangest transformation took place, so strange that he could not be clear in his head whether he was Christopher Sly, thumping-bag of hostesses and butt of angry females, asleep; a lord awake – or a piece of transparent air, and the dream of other watchers. The tapestried walls, the encrusted ceiling, the lady-wife and servants seemed to dissolve, and the great mansion itself to vanish; and in their place was magically the clear blue sky and rosy painted streets of an old Italian town!

It was sunny, bustling Padua, where rich old Baptista Minola had two daughters, one like an angel from heaven, and one from the other place. The last was Katherine, who had a tongue like burnt bacon, and a temper like mustard without beef. Bianca, the angel, had two suitors, which was not to be wondered at; Katherine, the elder, had none, which was not to be wondered at either. Their father would have given half his fortune to have got Katherine off his hands; and Bianca would have given the other half, because her father had determined that she could not marry unless someone married Katherine first. And that seemed as likely a happening as snow in hell. So they all walked along a street in Padua, Baptista between Bianca's two suitors, and his two daughters behind: Katherine looking daggers at the gentle and well-loved Bianca, and Bianca, who was more seemly and domestic, looking needles back.

Hopelessly old Baptista suggested that, if the suitors transferred their attentions to his eldest child, he would make it well worth their while. Vigorously the gentlemen shook their heads; which, though she would not have had either of them save on a roasting-dish with an apple in his mouth, did not please Katherine at all. Addressing herself to the younger (for the other was no better than an ancient money-bag in wrinkled stockings), she offered to "comb his noddle with a three-legged stool." Her father glared at her, and she glared back; and most decidedly got the better of the exchange.

"Go in, Bianca," said her father gently to his angel, for they stood outside his house. Bianca curtsied modestly, and, with a mildly reproachful look at her sister, withdrew to her books and music and suchlike maidenly pursuits. The suitors sighed; and Baptista asked if they knew of schoolmasters who might further improve Bianca, if such a thing were possible. While they thought about it, Baptista hurried into the house, saying, over his shoulder: "Katherina, you may stay," either in the hope that she and the gentleman would soften towards one another, or else just to make good his escape.

"Why, and I trust I may go too, may I not?" demanded Katherine, with a look that would have curdled ale. "Ha!" she cried; and went in after her father like a whirlwind, and slammed the door.

The suitors looked at one another. It was plain that, if they wished to prosper with Bianca, they would have to find a husband for Katherine first.

"There be good fellows in the world," said Hortensio, the younger, "would take her with all faults, and money enough."

They nodded, but with little conviction. Could there really be such a man?

"Would I had given him the best horse in Padua to begin his wooing," sighed the ancient money-bag, whose name was Gremio, "that would thoroughly woo her, wed her, and bed her, and rid the house of her!"

They shook their heads and departed, leaving the street quiet, save for in Baptista's house where doors kept going off like exploding chestnuts as Katherine stormed from room to room.

Two figures came out from a neighbouring doorway, where they had been silent lookers-on. They were from Pisa and strangers to Padua, and they marvelled greatly at what they had seen and heard. One was Lucentio, a young gentleman in colours so bright you might have cooked by them; the other was his servant Tranio, who wore long striped stockings, like barbers' poles, and a cap like a brace of pheasant. The servant looked at his master, and the master looked into air. His eyes were as round and bright as sixpences. He was spellbound! He had seen an angel, a gentle angel of loveliness! He had fallen in love with Bianca! Everything else fled from his brain. He quite forgot that he had come to Padua on business for his father. He could think of nothing but Bianca and how he might get to her.

He would disguise himself as a schoolmaster! He had heard her father say that he wanted masters for her.

"Not possible," said Tranio firmly: "for who shall bear your part and be in Padua here Vicentio's son?"

This was true. He was to have taken lodgings to entertain rich merchants for his father, Vicentio. He could not be in two places at once. He pondered; but not for long, for love lends wings to thought. He and Tranio would change about! Tranio would be Lucentio and entertain his father's friends, while he, Lucentio, would be a humble schoolmaster, teaching the fair Bianca Latin, Greek, and whatever more her modesty would allow. Tranio agreed, for deception ran in his veins like blood; so without more ado, man and master changed cloaks and hats, and were instantly transformed.

Hortensio, wracking his brains to think of some presentable fellow whose spirit was stout enough, and whose purse was lean enough, to try his fortunes with Katherine, walked slowly back to his house. He stopped. There was an argument in progress outside his gate. A sturdy young man was heartily thumping his companion, who was roaring for help. Hortensio smiled. One was Petruchio, a friend of his from Verona; the other was his friend's servant Grumio, who doubtless deserved what he was getting. He hastened to greet them and to ask Petruchio what he was doing in Padua.

"Such wind as scatters young men through the world," began Petruchio, in a fine and lofty style, for he was an excellent fellow and the best of comrades in an ale-house brawl; but then his face grew solemn, and an anxious look haunted his eyes. His father had died and had left him, to put it plainly, somewhat short of money. "Crowns in my purse I have, and goods at home," he said hastily, as if to reassure Hortensio that he had not come to borrow money. "I come," he said with utter honesty, "to wive it wealthily in Padua . . ."

Hortensio's heart quickened. Could his prayers have been answered so pat? Cautiously he mentioned that he knew of a lady who was very rich. Then he shook his head. She had disadvantages. "Thou'rt too much my friend," he said regretfully, "I'll not wish thee to her."

But Petruchio was not so easily put off. What was wrong with the lady? A sharp tongue and a bad temper? "Think you a little din can daunt mine ears?" he demanded bravely. "Have I not in my time heard lions roar?"

Hortensio shook his head. "I would not wed her," he said, "for a mine of gold."

"Thou know'st not gold's effect," said Petruchio bitterly, having discovered the evil of need and thinking peace a small price to pay to be rid of it. "Tell me her father's name and 'tis enough . . ."

"Her father is Baptista Minola," said Hortensio, seeing that nothing would shake his friend's resolve; and went on to tell him everything, even that he himself hoped to marry the younger daughter when Katherine had been taken off her father's hands.

"I know her father," nodded Petruchio; and this turned out to be a great convenience to Hortensio, who promptly asked a favour. When Petruchio called on old Baptista he should take with him a certain schoolmaster and recommend him warmly as an instructor to Bianca. This schoolmaster would, of course, be Hortensio himself in an impenetrable disguise.

Readily, Petruchio agreed; but before anything could be done, Bianca's other suitor, the ancient Gremio appeared. And he was not alone. By the strangest chance, he had found a schoolmaster for Bianca, a pleasant enough looking fellow, but no better dressed than a tinker on Sunday. He said his name was Cambio, but anyone who knew him could have seen, with half an eye, that he was Lucentio in disguise.

Hortensio, annoyed that his rival should have forestalled him in the business of schoolmasters, remarked that he, too, had found a learned person; but, what was more to the point, he had also found someone willing to court Katherine. He pointed to Petruchio. Gremio peered at him incredulously.

"Hortensio," he asked quietly, "have you told him all her faults?"

"I know she is an irksome brawling scold," said Petruchio.

Gremio shrugged his shoulders. "If you have a stomach," he said, "to it a God's name! you shall have me assisting you in all."

Then Hortensio, finding himself lagging behind Gremio yet again, made the same offer; and Petruchio sighed with relief. He had been wondering where the money would come from to pay the cost of wooing.

They were preparing to set off for Baptista's house, when matters took yet another turn. A personage in a brightly coloured cloak and hat, came mincing down the street like a sunburst. He greeted them ceremoniously, and announced himself as yet another suitor to the fair Bianca. The two rivals were indignant. Who was this impudent newcomer? He declared that he was one Lucentio of Pisa, and very rich; though anyone with half an eye could have seen that he was Tranio in his master's clothes, and guessed that his master had put him up to it; but they believed him.

"Did you yet ever see Baptista's daughter?" demanded Hortensio.

"No, sir," replied Tranio; but he had heard that she was beautiful and wealthy, and that was enough for him.

The rivals looked at one another. They sighed. Honey-sweet Bianca was gathering suitors like bees. They had no right to send the new one away, but, nonetheless, he ought to pay his share towards the cost of getting rid of that fierce impediment, Katherine. "You must," said Hortensio, gesturing towards Petruchio, "as we do, gratify this gentleman . . ."

Tranio, cheerfully making free with his master's

money, agreed. Petruchio beamed. He felt a new man. But those who knew better, felt that Katherine would soon make an old one of him.

The door of Baptista's house flew open, and out came Bianca, weeping like April with the fury of March close behind. Her sister, by means of horrible threats and superior strength, had tied her hands together and pushed her out into the street. Loudly she jeered at Bianca for her suitors, while gentle Bianca wept and meekly pleaded to be set free.

"You have but jested with me all this while," she ventured, smiling bravely through her tears. "I prithee, sister Kate, untie my hands."

Katherine hit her, bringing down her hair like a tumbled sheaf of corn. Bianca shrieked; and out of the house came Baptista. He saw his angel bound and weeping, and was outraged. Tenderly he untied her and demanded of her cruel persecutor: "When did she cross thee with a bitter word?"

"Her silence flouts me!" answered Katherine, and, with upraised fists, flew at her sister yet again.

"Bianca, get thee in!" urged Baptista, stepping hastily between his children and allowing Bianca to escape.

"I see she is your treasure!" shouted Katherine; and, her breast heaving with indignation, she rushed away to weep and plot revenge.

"Was ever gentleman thus grieved as I?" groaned Baptista; and then hurriedly composed himself for visitors were approaching.

They were Signor Gremio, Bianca's elderly suitor, smiling like a crumpled face in a tapestry, with some half dozen strangers, all of whom were smiling too. But then, why not? The sun was bright and, doubtless, none of them had daughters. Then the morning, which had begun so stormily for Baptista, turned radiant!

Not only had that good Signor Gremio brought him a schoolmaster for Bianca, wise in Latin and Greek, but also, and most marvellously, a suitor for Katherine! He was a fine-looking young fellow by name of Petruchio of Verona. Baptista had known his father, so he was no idle scrap of nonsense off the streets. On the contrary, he was well-dressed and courteous, and had inquired most civilly: "Pray have you not a daughter called Katherina, fair and virtuous?"

"I have a daughter, sir," Baptista had responded, "called Katherina," and had left it at that. He did not wish to misrepresent his eldest child; particularly as none could fail to hear her stormy passage through the house. But Petruchio was not put off; and he, too, had brought a schoolmaster, skilled in music and mathematics, whom he offered like an academic bouquet. Baptista stared. He had never seen a more learned looking man in all his life. Solemnly gowned in black, he peered out at the world through spectacles as thick as bottles and he was whiskered like a broom. A man like that must have had a whole university in his head!

Baptista was delighted; but his morning's good fortune was not over yet. Another the strangers, a young gentleman in a brightly coloured hat and cloak, bowed low and presented himself as Lucentio of Pisa, who was enormously rich. It was his earnest desire to be numbered among the suitors to the fair Bianca, and he pressed upon Baptista, with his best wishes, a pudding-faced boy bearing a pile of Greek and Latin volumes, and a lute.

What a morning! Baptista, who had never before got anything by having daughters, save aggravation and distress, now found himself the happy possessor of two more suitors – one for each child – two schoolmasters, and the instruments of their craft! And all in a matter of minutes! Beaming, he despatched lute, books and scholars into his house, so that his daughters' improvement might begin without delay. Then he turned eagerly to Petruchio to settle the matter of Katherine's dowry, before the young man could change his mind.

"Well mayst thou woo," said Baptista, warmly shaking Petruchio by the hand when matters were settled, "and happy be thy speed . . ." Then his hope of seeing his eldest daughter married and in Verona, received a set-back.

The door burst open and out staggered Petruchio's learned gift. He was clutching his brow, which was decorated with a lute-string and splinters of wood. Katherine had broken his lute over his head.

Baptista sighed; and, comforting the dazed scholar as best he could, prepared to lead him back into the house to try for better things with the gentle Bianca. "Signor Petruchio," he asked uncomfortably, "will you go with us, or shall I send my daughter Kate to you?"

"I pray you do," said Petruchio; and off went the father, marvelling greatly.

Kate came out. She was divided between anger at having been sent for, and curiosity to see why. She had never had a suitor before, and she did not like the look of him. He smirked at her as if she was a joint of lamb.

"Good morrow, Kate, for that's your name, I hear," he said.

"Well have you heard, but something hard of hearing," she answered coldly; "they call me Katherine that do talk of me."

"You lie, in faith," said he, returning her cold look with a warm one, "for you are called plain Kate, and bonny Kate, and sometimes Kate the curst; but Kate, the prettiest Kate in Christendom!" He spoke the truth, for she was indeed beautiful; and when he concluded by saying: "Myself am moved to woo thee for my wife," he meant it.

She replied, contemptuously. He countered amiably. She frowned; he smiled. She called him an ass; he called her a woman. She told him to be off.

"Nay, come again," said he, "good Kate, I am a gentleman – "

"That I'll try!" she cried, and hit him as hard as she could.

"I swear I'll cuff you," said Petruchio, rubbing his burning cheek and keeping his temper with difficulty, "if you strike again."

She scowled; and lowered her hand.

"Nay, come, Kate, come," said he, coaxingly, "you must not look so sour."

"It is my fashion when I see a crab," she answered; and so the courtship proceeded, sweet as vinegar, and gentle as a raging sea: she the wind, and he the mariner fighting to contain her blasts.

"Now, Kate, I am a husband for your turn!" he panted, pinioning her arms and struggling to avoid her kicks. "I am he am born to tame you, Kate, and bring you from a wild Kate to a Kate conformable as other household Kates!"

Suddenly he set her free; her father was coming, together with Bianca's suitors.

"Now, Signor Petruchio," inquired Baptista, looking uneasily from flushed face to flushed and glaring face, "how speed you with my daughter?"

"How but well, sir?" responded Petruchio, to the father's relief. "How but well?"

"Why, how now, daughter Katherine?" asked Baptista tenderly, perceiving that his eldest child looked somewhat despondent. "In your dumps?"

"Call you me daughter?" shrieked Katherine, and went on to abuse the poor man for daring to thrust her upon, as she put it, "one half lunatic, a madcap ruffian and a swearing Jack!" She pointed a trembling finger at Petruchio, so there should be no mistake about who she meant.

Father and suitors looked dismayed; but Petruchio, with the utmost cheerfulness assured them that all was well. He and Kate had agreed that, in company she should be perverse, while in private they were the best of lovers. Furthermore, matters had proceeded so swiftly between them, that he was off to Venice to buy wedding clothes, for they were to be married on Sunday!

"And kiss me, Kate!" he cried, seizing the speechless Katherine round the waist and holding her tightly: "We will be married o' Sunday!" Then he whirled her away, leaving father and suitors overwhelmed with joy.

"Faith, gentlemen, now I play a merchant's part," said Baptista, addressing himself to Bianca's suitors; for now it remained only for him to dispose of his other child.

Gremio, by reason of having been first in the field, claimed the prior right; but Tranio, in his master's hat and cloak, claimed a better love. Gremio sneered at his rival for being too young; and Tranio jeered at Gremio for being too old. So Baptista, exercising his rights of judgement, declared that Bianca's love was a prize to be won, not by words but by deeds. Whoever offered most should have her. Gleefully Gremio rushed in with a list of his considerable property, all of which he was willing to make over to Bianca. Tranio, with the reckless generosity of one who promises in another's name, outbid him to the tune of two more houses and two thousand ducats a year. Gremio staggered, but bravely came up with more land and an argosy in Marseilles. Then Tranio sank him with three argosies, and a whole fleet besides. Gremio was finished, and the father shook the victor by the hand. "Your offer is the best," he said, affectionately; "and let your father make her the assurance, she is your own."

Bianca was learning Latin. While the sage of music and mathematics watched suspiciously from the other side of the room, and twangled on his new lute, Bianca's head was bent so close to the other sage's, that she might have got knowledge through seepage. They murmured low; and it was wonderful, Bianca discovered, what interesting meanings might be got from Ovid. For instance, when Penelope wrote to Ulysses, she saw fit to tell him that her name was Lucentio, son of Vicentio of Pisa, that he had disguised himself to make love to her, and that his man Tranio was disguised as himself in order to get rid of old Gremio.

Bianca nodded, and, learning fast, translated the same passage again, when it appeared that Penelope wrote to tell Ulysses that ... she knew him not, that she trusted him not, that he was to speak soft lest the musical sage overheard them; and that he was not to give up hope. She smiled, and he smiled, and Ovid, had he known the use to which his work had been put, would not have been displeased.

Next came the turn of the music master; and he did not lag far behind. He instructed his fair pupil in the scale, which, in accordance with a new system of fingering, invented by himself, revealed that her whiskered and bottled-eyed teacher was Hortensio in disguise, that he loved her, and that he would surely perish if she refused him.

"Tut! I like it not!" said Bianca, pushing aside the mysteriously legible lute. "Old fashions please me best. I am not so nice, to change true rules for odd inventions." She gazed fondly at the Latinist, and Hortensio scowled.

* * *

Kate's wedding Sunday had come, and was nearly gone; and it had been a day that neither bride, nor bride's people, nor priest nor sexton nor church itself was ever likely to forget. And not on account of joy.

The groom was late, so late that it was feared he would not come. Kate was thrown into an agony of mortification, for the shame of being abandoned was worse than the shame of being married. Then he came, and it would have been better if he hadn't; for the shame of being married turned out to be ten times worse than shame of being left. Petruchio came to his wedding in rags and rubbish, in old patched clothes, odd boots and a broken sword, and he rode upon a horse that could scarcely stagger.

"Good sooth," said he in surprise, when his attire was called into question, "to me she's married, not unto my clothes."

But all this was no more than a mild prologue to the wedding itself. When asked if he would take Katherine for his wife, he answered so loud and with such swearing, that the priest dropped the book in amazement; and Petruchio cuffed him soundly as he bent to pick it up! After which, he called for wine, drank some, and threw the rest over the sexton. "This done," related the shocked Gremio, who had been witness to everything, "he took the bride about the neck, and kissed her lips with such a clamorous smack that at the parting all the church did echo!"

It had indeed been a wedding to remember, with a mad bridegroom and a bride so terrified that she dared not speak for fear of what might happen next. Then came the wedding feast, which was over before it had begun. Petruchio would not stay, and Katherine would not go. "Do what thou canst," she said, "I will not go today." She turned to the wedding guests. "Gentlemen, forward to the bridal dinner . . ."

"They shall go forward, Kate, at thy command,"

agreed Petruchio. "But for my bonny Kate, she must with me!" Then, seizing her round the waist, and waving his battered sword as if to defy all the world, he heaved her out of the house!

The wedding guests stared at the violently swinging door. Some smiled, some laughed, some rose to follow. "Nay, let them go," said old Baptista, more frightened of his daughter than for her; "a couple of quiet ones."

The journey to Petruchio's house was long, hard and muddy; and, when bride and bridegroom arrived, Kate was faint and quiet from weariness and hunger. But Petruchio was in the best of spirits. He sang, and cuffed his servants and swore at them, and, in general, behaved as if he was back in church.

"Sit down, Kate," he roared, "and welcome! Food, food, food, food!"

Kate regarded her shabby husband and his shabby house with hatred; nonetheless, she sat, for hunger was a strict master, even over the most turbulent of spirits.

Food came, and Kate brightened; but alas! the food was not to Petruchio's liking. It was ill-prepared and burnt; and he flung it back in his servants' faces. "Be patient," he said to his enraged and starving bride. "Tomorrow't shall be mended, and for this night we'll fast for company. Come, I will bring thee to thy bridal chamber." She went as mildly as a tiger, and with such a look that those who saw it might have supposed she meant to dine upon her husband as he slept.

Petruchio smiled. He had got Kate's dowry, but now he was greedy and wanted more. He wanted her heart as well. But Kate's heart, like gold or any precious thing, was buried deep, and needed mining for, with strength and resolution, and loud explosions. Accordingly he kept her awake all night, with lectures and complaints about the ill-made bed.

* * *

Hortensio was disgusted. Bianca, in spite of her claim to be pleased by old fashions, had turned from him, the seasoned admirer, and bestowed her favours on the wretched young teacher of Latin. Bitterly he had watched them exchange looks and sighs, and steal sly kisses, like furtive apples. At length, he could endure it no longer; and his deathless love, for want of fuel, flickered and died. There was a rich widow he knew, and he would marry her; but first he would go to see how his friend Petruchio was faring, with his fierce Kate. As whiskers, spectacles and lutes had done him no good, he felt he had much to learn before he tried again.

Petruchio's wife was not well pleased.

"Mistress, what cheer?" inquired Hortensio, cautiously.

"Faith, as cold as can be," came the bitter reply. She was hungry. Her husband, all concern, brought her food he had prepared himself. She looked at it, as if it might vanish before her eyes.

"What, not a word?" asked Petruchio, disappointed by the reception of his efforts. "Nay then, thou love'st it not. Here, take away this dish."

"I pray you, let it stand," cried Katherine quickly, her bright tongue moistening her eager lips.

"The poorest service is repaid with thanks," said Petruchio

"I thank you, sir," said Katherine; and Hortensio stared.

She began to eat, as one who has not eaten for many days; but was stopped, it seemed, almost as soon as she had begun. A tailor came in, laden with rich gowns for the lady. Kate eyed them with interest; but Petruchio was enraged. Everything the tailor showed was at fault. There was nothing, in all his stock, that was good enough for Kate.

"I never saw a better fashioned gown," pleaded

Katherine, as the tailor displayed the choicest garment she had seen.

"He means to make a puppet of thee!" said Petruchio contemptuously; and dismissed the tailor and all his wares. "Well, come, my Kate," he said, comfortingly, "we will unto your father's even in these honest mean habiliments. 'Tis the mind that makes the body rich."

Kate's eyes filled with tears. Her gown was the gown she had come in, and was somewhat the worse for wear. Petruchio called for horses, for it was in his mind to set out directly for Padua and old Baptista's house.

"Let's see," he said, "I think 'tis now some seven o'clock . . ."

"I dare assure you, sir," corrected Kate, "'tis almost two . . ."

Petruchio frowned. "It shall be what o'clock I say it is."

"Why," murmured Hortensio, shaking his head, "so this gallant will command the sun!"

And so he did, upon the long and tedious journey back to Padua.

"Good Lord!" he cried out suddenly. "How bright and goodly shines the moon!"

"The moon? The sun!" protested Kate. "It is not moonlight now."

"I say it is the moon!"

"I know it is the sun."

"It shall be moon, or star, or what I list," said Petruchio firmly; "Or e'er I journey to your father's house."

"Say as he says," pleaded Hortensio, "or we shall never go."

Kate sighed. She was aching and weary; and she had suffered much, she reflected, as she had made others suffer. It would be folly to suffer more. It was the moon if he wanted it to be the moon, or a candle if he preferred. It was the wiser course, she thought, to deny the evidence of her senses, than her good sense.

"What you will have it named," she said, "even that it is, and so it shall be so for Katherine." She looked at him. He was a plain, rough fellow who had weathered her storms. He was, she felt, a mariner to be admired. She smiled at him; and he tried hard not to smile back.

"Petruchio," said Hortensio softly, "go thy ways, the field is won."

There was a great celebration in old Baptista's house, a wedding feast of huge proportions. It was a feast to celebrate a triple marriage: Lucentio, as himself at last, and books and scholarship thrown to the winds, had got Baptista's blessing and gentle Bianca's hand. Hortensio had briskly courted and married the widow, who sat beside him, as ripe and tempting as an orchard of plums. And Kate and Petruchio, who, though married once, seemed now married again, heart to heart.

"Nothing but sit and sit, and eat and eat!" cried Petruchio, with a cheerful and knowing look to his wife. The talk was free and merry, and presently the ladies withdrew. Then the gentlemen talked of the good fortune they had in their wives; until old Baptista, overcome with wine and sympathy, leaned over and laid his arm consolingly upon the shoulder of the husband of his eldest child. "Now, in good sadness, son Petruchio," he wept, "I think thou hast the veriest shrew of all."

Gently Petruchio set his father-in-law upright. "Well, I say no," he said; for he would not rate his Katherine below her sister or Hortensio's plump bride. Indeed, he rated her far above them; so much so that he was willing to wager a hundred crowns on Kate's proving superior in courtesy and duty. Each husband was to send for his wife; and whichever came first should take the prize.

"Who shall begin?" cried Hortensio.

"That will I," said Lucentio, whose bride was an angel of gentleness. He sent his boy to fetch her, and smiled confidently as he waited.

The boy returned. "My mistress sends you word," he said uncomfortably, "she is busy and she cannot come."

"Is that an answer?" asked Petruchio, gravely.

"Pray God," said old Gremio, between mouthfuls, "your wife send you not a worse."

Petruchio shrugged his shoulders, and waited while Hortensio sent the boy to fetch the widow. He returned almost as soon as he'd gone.

"She will not come," was the message. "She bids you come to her."

"Worse and worse!" cried Petruchio, shocked beyond measure. "Go to your mistress," he bade his servant. "Say I command her come to me."

"I know her answer," said Hortensio, when the servant had gone.

"What?"

"She will not."

The table nodded sagely, when old Baptista cried out: "Now, by my holidame, here comes Katherina!"

Kate came in, looked about her, saw amazement on every face, save on her husband's. "What is your will, sir, that you send for me?" she asked.

"Where is your sister and Hortensio's wife?"

"They sit conferring by the parlour fire," answered Kate, trying not to smile.

"Go fetch them hither," commanded Petruchio; and waited for the errant ladies to appear.

"Now fair befall thee, good Petruchio!" cried old Baptista, through rosy clouds of wine; and he offered a second dowry with Katherina, for surely she was a new Kate.

The new Kate came, and, smiling, made a pleasant

contrast with the peevish looks of the ladies she had fetched.

"Katherine, I charge thee," said Petruchio, "tell these headstrong women what duty they do owe their lords and husbands."

"Come, come, you're mocking," protested Hortensio's wife, "we will have no telling!"

But they did; and most eloquently. Kate bade them consider what they owed their husbands, for safety, security and comfort; and then to consider how little they were asked in return. Or was obedience to another's wishes so demeaning a thing? "My mind hath been as big as one of yours," she said, "my heart as great, my reason haply more, to bandy word for word and frown for frown." She shook her head. Such warfare profited none. Then, with a sudden gesture, she knelt and placed her hand beneath her husband's foot.

All were silent. The gesture had not humbled Kate; but had raised her husband because it showed that he was high in her esteem.

"Why, there's a wench!" cried Petruchio, in admiration. "Come on, and kiss me, Kate!" He had begun his courting with a love of coin; but now he knew no greater riches than the coins of love.

"Come, Kate, we'll to bed," he said, and led her gently away. One by one the others followed, until the feasting chamber was empty and in darkness.

All was silent, save for a sound of soft snores. Was it a sleeping reveller; or was it a sleeping tinker, all alone?

HEINEMANN NEW WINDMILLS

Founding Editors: Anne and Ian Serraillier

Chinua Achebe Things Fall Apart
Douglas Adams The Hitchhiker's Guide to the Galaxy
Vivien Alcock The Cuckoo Sister; The Monster Garden; The Trial of Anna Cotman; A Kind of Thief
Margaret Atwood The Handmaid's Tale
J G Ballard Empire of the Sun
Nina Bawden The Witch's Daughter; A Handful of Thieves; Carrie's War; The Robbers; Devil by the Sea; Kept in the Dark; The Finding; Keeping Henry; Humbug
E R Braithwaite To Sir, With Love
John Branfield The Day I Shot My Dad
F Hodgson Burnett The Secret Garden
Ray Bradbury The Golden Apples of the Sun; The Illustrated Man
Betsy Byars The Midnight Fox; Goodbye, Chicken Little; The Pinballs
Victor Canning The Runaways; Flight of the Grey Goose
Ann Coburn Welcome to the Real World
Hannah Cole Bring in the Spring
Jane Leslie Conly Racso and the Rats of NIMH
Robert Cormier We All Fall Down
Roald Dahl Danny, The Champion of the World; The Wonderful Story of Henry Sugar; George's Marvellous Medicine; The BFG; The Witches; Boy; Going Solo; Charlie and the Chocolate Factory; Matilda
Anita Desai The Village by the Sea
Charles Dickens A Christmas Carol; Great Expectations
Peter Dickinson The Gift; Annerton Pit; Healer
Berlie Doherty Granny was a Buffer Girl
Gerald Durrell My Family and Other Animals
J M Falkner Moonfleet
Anne Fine The Granny Project
Anne Frank The Diary of Anne Frank
Leon Garfield Six Apprentices
Jamila Gavin The Wheel of Surya
Adele Geras Snapshots of Paradise

Graham Greene The Third Man and The Fallen Idol; Brighton Rock

Thomas Hardy The Withered Arm and Other Wessex Tales

Rosemary Harris Zed

L P Hartley The Go-Between

Ernest Hemingway The Old Man and the Sea; A Farewell to Arms

Nat Hentoff Does this School have Capital Punishment?

Nigel Hinton Getting Free; Buddy; Buddy's Song

Minfong Ho Rice Without Rain

Anne Holm I Am David

Janni Howker Badger on the Barge; Isaac Campion

Linda Hoy Your Friend Rebecca

Barbara Ireson (Editor) In a Class of Their Own

Jennifer Johnston Shadows on Our Skin

Toeckey Jones Go Well, Stay Well

James Joyce A Portrait of the Artist as a Young Man

Geraldine Kaye Comfort Herself; A Breath of Fresh Air

Clive King Me and My Million

Dick King-Smith The Sheep-Pig

Daniel Keyes Flowers for Algernon

Elizabeth Laird Red Sky in the Morning; Kiss the Dust

D H Lawrence The Fox and The Virgin and the Gypsy; Selected Tales

Harper Lee To Kill a Mockingbird

Julius Lester Basketball Game

Ursula Le Guin A Wizard of Earthsea

C Day Lewis The Otterbury Incident

David Line Run for Your Life; Screaming High

Joan Lingard Across the Barricades; Into Exile; The Clearance; The File on Fraulein Berg

Penelope Lively The Ghost of Thomas Kempe

Jack London The Call of the Wild; White Fang

Bernard Mac Laverty Cal; The Best of Bernard Mac Laverty

Margaret Mahy The Haunting; The Catalogue of The Universe

Jan Mark Do You Read Me? Eight Short Stories

James Vance Marshall Walkabout

Somerset Maugham The Kite and Other Stories

Michael Morpurgo Waiting for Anya; My Friend Walter; The War of Jenkins' Ear

How many have you read?